This year WHSmith celebrates its 225th anniversary and to mark this momentous occasion, we are pledging to raise £2 million split between three charities: Cancer Research UK, Mind and the National Literacy Trust.

Several authors have kindly agreed to supply WHSmith with exclusive short stories, in order to enable us to offer customers something new to the market and to donate £1 from each sale, split equally between the chosen charities.

We do hope you enjoy reading these specially chosen titles and join us in thanking the authors for their support.

Sandra Bradley
Trading Controller
Fiction Books

KU-175-624

Carole Matthews is the *Sunday Times* bestselling author of twenty-nine novels, including the Top Ten bestsellers *The Cake Shop in the Garden*, *A Cottage by the Sea*, *The Chocolate Lovers' Christmas* and *The Chocolate Lovers' Wedding*. In 2015, Carole was awarded the RNA Outstanding Achievement Award. Her novels dazzle and delight readers all over the world. She is published in more than thirty countries and her books have sold to Hollywood.

For all the latest news from Carole, visit **www.carolematthews.com**, follow Carole on Twitter (**@carolematthews**) and Instagram (**matthews.carole**) or join the thousands of readers who have become Carole's friend on Facebook (**carolematthewsbooks**).

Also by Carole Matthews

Let's Meet on Platform 8

A Whiff of Scandal

More to Life Than This

For Better, For Worse

A Minor Indiscretion

A Compromising Position

The Sweetest Taboo

With or Without You

You Drive Me Crazy

Welcome to the Real World

It's a Kind of Magic

All You Need is Love

The Difference a Day Makes

That Loving Feeling

It's Now or Never

The Only Way is Up

Wrapped Up in You

Summer Daydreams

With Love at Christmas

A Cottage by the Sea

Calling Mrs Christmas

A Place to Call Home

The Christmas Party

The Cake Shop in the Garden

Paper Hearts
and Summer Kisses

Christmas Cakes
and Mistletoe Nights

The Chocolate Lovers Novels

The Chocolate Lovers' Club

The Chocolate Lovers' Diet

The Chocolate Lovers' Christmas

The Chocolate Lovers' Wedding

Carole Matthews

Sunshine with a Chance of Snow

and other stories

sphere

SPHERE

Individual stories first published in Great Britain in 2013 as ebooks by Sphere
This collection first published in 2017 by Sphere

3 5 7 9 10 8 6 4 2

A CIP catalogue record for this book is available from the British Library.

ISBN 978-0-7515-7070-0

Typeset in Sabon LT Std by Palimpsest Book Productions Ltd,
Falkirk, Stirlingshire

Printed and bound in Great Britain by Clays Ltd, St Ives plc

Papers used by Sphere are from well-managed forests
and other responsible sources.

Sphere
An imprint of
Little, Brown Book Group
Carmelite House
50 Victoria Embankment
London
EC4Y 0DZ

An Hachette UK Company
www.hachette.co.uk

www.littlebrown.co.uk

Introduction

Over the years I've loved writing short stories and it was due to a happy accident resulting from a short story that I got my first break in publishing.

Back in the day – about 1995 – I entered the annual Love Story Competition in a publication called *Writing Magazine*. I was buying it as I was writing factual pieces about aromatherapy at the time and was looking for tips and market leads. I'd spent a long time writing about bad backs and so forth for various publications as a freelance writer and perhaps I was ready for a change. I really had no intention of writing fiction, yet something about this competition piqued my interest and I thought I'd give it a go.

So I wrote a story called *Ignorance is Bliss* and it was the first fiction I'd attempted since I'd been coerced into doing essays for my school homework. Fittingly, it's also the first story in this collection and it's a sad and slightly twisted tale of infidelity. I was quite pleased with it for an initial effort and felt confident enough to send it off, though I had nothing to measure it against. A few weeks later and to my complete amazement – and everyone else's – I won a thousand pounds from The David Thomas Charitable Trust for my endeavour.

Flushed with success, I then did the most sensible thing I've ever done in my life. Instead of splashing out with my prize money on shoes and handbags, as is my usual style, I spent the money on a writing course.

As the course approached, I thought that I should start a novel and, by the time I walked through the doors a couple of months later, I'd finished about half of it. I spent a week there and we'd write during the day and read out our work after dinner. The tutor on the course loved my book and suggested that I finish it straightaway and send it to an agent. I took her advice and did just that. By Christmas that year, it was completed and I'd posted it off. The first week in the new year, the agent phoned me and asked to take me on as a client. Every writer needs a bit of good luck and a following wind and I was fortunate enough to catch the start of the whole 'chick-lit' thing and the agent sold it within a week. I couldn't believe how quickly it all moved. That book became my first novel, *Let's Meet on Platform 8*, published in 1997.

Even now, if I have a day where my current work-in-progress isn't flowing all that well, I'll put it to one side and write a short story instead. I find writing them really relaxing and fun. Sometimes a little snapshot is all that's needed. I don't keep a journal, but whenever I've travelled or had a poignant moment in my life, I've often found that writing a short story is a great way to capture them. Each one of these tales is special to me for a different reason and has lovely memories.

So, kick off your shoes, curl up on the sofa – preferably with chocolate and a glass of something nice – ignore the housework and take half an hour to enjoy these short stories.

Love, Carole :) xx

Ignorance is Bliss is the first short story I ever wrote and it won me a lovely prize. It's a bit darker than my usual writing style and, with the benefit of experience, I'd probably do it a differently now, but I hope you enjoy it. It will always have a special place in my heart as it's this little story that started me on a career that was to span twenty-nine books and twenty years. Who knew?

It states on the very smart First Prize certificate I was presented with: *It is hoped that those who achieve success in their competitions will go on to further distinction and perhaps themselves be able to offer help to other writers one day.*

I hope I can say I've done that.

Ignorance is Bliss

To Pamela, Happy birthday, darling. It's your secretary's writing. I know it well by now. Instantly, I recognise the over-exaggerated curve of her letters and the way she hesitates in the middle of my name as if she can't quite bring herself to write it. She's sent me another bouquet. I hate bouquets. Dead flowers. Their sweet, sickly scent never quite manages to mask the all-pervading stench of a decaying marriage.

Dutifully, I arrange them in a vase, ready for your approval when you arrive home. I put them in the centre of the dining room table, where we'll eat our romantic candlelit supper for two. The meal is very special, all your favourite dishes, no expense spared. Nothing is too good for you. I've spent all afternoon preparing it. We'll drink a bottle of rare vintage wine and laugh together. And we'll both be disappointed that we are not somewhere else.

You don't know how much the flowers have cost, but your secretary will give you the Mastercard slip, eventually. She'll lean close against you as you grace the bill with your signature. We'll both look at the flowers and think of her. I know her name, but I always refer to her as 'your secretary' and so do you. It's a pretty name and you're afraid that you'll speak it more tenderly than you should. It sticks in my throat like the bitter taste of bile. So we keep it impersonal.

She chooses me quite nice presents, really. Not exactly the

style or quality I'd choose for myself but acceptable, nevertheless. After three years her taste has improved considerably. She doesn't know I hate flowers though. Or perhaps she does. I never wear the presents she buys and you never ask me why, despite the expense. Casually, I discard them all in a box at the bottom of my wardrobe where they gather dust. They are the first thing I see every morning when I choose my clothes for the day.

It's time-consuming, being married to an unfaithful husband. Before I can do the laundry each item has to be scrutinised for stains. Nothing so obvious as lipstick on the collar, darling — even you are more discreet than that. But tiny, minute, tell-tale marks that speak of illicit unions. The sort of evidence that you wouldn't notice as clothes were flung hastily to the floor in the frenzy of passion or as you dress hurriedly, carelessly after your snatched sessions of love-making. At home your trousers are always meticulously hung and they are never creased. I examine every crumple in your shirts. I notice them all. I store them in my memory.

Women are more careful. If she has someone waiting for her at home a woman will never rush breathlessly through the door, her hair tousled from tumbling in bed. She'll make sure that the scarlet flush of lust has faded from her breasts, her throat and her face before she presents herself once more as a loving wife. Her hair will be as smooth as her composure. Her lipstick, seduced from her lips by countless crushing kisses, will be re-applied immaculately. Women leave no signs.

I know the secret number for the combination lock on your briefcase, so I have to go through your diary and all your documents to find out where you will be and with whom. Sometimes I play tricks on you and leave it unlocked after my pillage, so that you can never be quite sure whether I've discovered your secrets or whether you've just been careless. You pride yourself on your caution. I have to open every sealed letter that I find hidden in your suits – suits that smell of your faded aftershave entwined with a hint of her perfume. Each pocket screams of opportunities to conceal your infidelities. Locked drawers have to be picked open to reveal their contents or extensive searches undertaken for concealed keys. Occasionally, you change your hiding places and make life more difficult for me. I check the last number redial on all the telephones to see if you've called her from our home. Sometimes you have and I listen to her voice when she answers the telephone, but I don't speak. This worries her. I can hear the distress edging into her sweet, sugary voice and this pleases me.

All these things take time. While you're on the golf course or at the squash club, relaxing and socialising, I'm busy steaming open your envelopes, burgling your property and probing into the life of your mistress so that they can be a part of my life too.

Many secretaries ago, when I was still naive and so desperately in love with you, I followed you to a hotel – a cold, impersonal tower block in the city on a freezing, rain-lashed day. But that didn't dampen your desire. I watched you both emerge onto the busy street, oblivious to the crowds of bad-tempered commuters pushing past you, cursing your intimacy. You embraced each other like love-struck teenagers, draping your bodies together, consciously sensual. She clung to the words on your love-swollen lips, silent words to my ears, mouthed only for her. And you laughed deep into each other's eyes. You gallantly covered her with your umbrella, protecting her from the onslaught. The icy fingers of rain swiped the tears from my face and threw them mockingly to the wind. I stood rooted to the floor, paralysed by your palpable passion. My hopes, my pride, my dreams and my love seeped out from me to be diluted for ever by the puddles at my feet. Since that day, I've never again followed you. Your diary is my eye into your world. Yet I'm driven, always, to see your mistresses. When they're alone. I resist it for as long as I can.

I discovered that, for once, your secretary wasn't going with you on your business trip last week. So I went to see her. She didn't see me. You don't suspect it, but I'm also capable of deceit. I sent her a bouquet. To the office. A bouquet of red roses. Dead red roses. Then I waited outside all afternoon, so that I'd see her when she went home. She's very diligent in her job: even though you were away she didn't leave early. Unfortunately, she was one of the last to leave and I was getting cold, the chill from the pavement eating into me and turning me to stone. But, at last, I saw her.

She pushes through the swing doors, the red roses clutched to her pert breasts, her hips swinging freely. Her smile is radiant and her cheeks are flushed. It's obvious she thinks the roses are from you. She should know by now that you don't send flowers. You only sign the bills.

I went back the next day at lunchtime and followed her. She buys trashy magazines to fill her long, lonely hours without you. I stood next to her as she queued for sandwiches. Tuna and mayonnaise. An excess of calories to caress her slender hips. She's ignorant of the sin of food and she has no need to control the things that enter her body. Not yet.

She looked at me without recognition – clearly, you have no photographs of me on your desk – and smiled politely. My stare would have frozen flame and she looked away hurt, confused and puzzled. I watched the sun play on her thick auburn hair, sending flashes of light through it. I inhaled deeply and the cloying smell of her perfume invaded my nostrils and imbedded itself for ever in my brain. So that wherever I go and whatever I do, whenever I smell that perfume it will always remind me of her. As it does you. I think I'll buy myself some and when

I want to torture you I'll drown myself in it and wrap myself around you. You'll lie in bed, making love to me, your wife, and you'll think of her. Her scent will wash over you like waves on a beach. But, after the first tingling crest enlivens you, the grains of sand will bite and scrape at your body until it bleeds.

Even after all these years you can't disguise your extra-marital relations. You are no longer relaxed enough to give me even a perfunctory peck on the cheek when you eventually arrive home, drawn and gaunt with exhaustion. It takes a lot of energy to lead a licentious life. Instead your first task is to absolve yourself from your sins. You let the healing power of steaming water stream over your nakedness, washing away her muskiness from your skin, cleansing your soul and your cheating body. The shower is your confessional and this is your daily act of contrition. Only then are you ready to face me.

You'll never leave me. I make your life too comfortable. You think I'm the dutiful wife, doting and unsuspecting. I make sure everything in your life looks flawless to the outside world. We are the perfect couple and our act has stood the test of many performances.

When the guilt becomes too much for you to bear, you buy me beautiful things for my beautiful house and expensive trinkets to adorn my firm, lean body. This massages your ego and assuages your guilt. Yet there's no need to worry, darling. I'll never divorce you. We are bound together eternally in our unholy union and I have guilt enough for both of us. For I know why every line has been etched deep at the corners of your eyes and what has caused every grey hair that frames your handsome face. I'm aware of your every move, every infidelity, every adulterous liaison. But you, my darling, are blissfully unaware of mine.

Some years ago, my partner, Lovely Kev, and I took a wonderful trip across China. One of the highlights was an overnight train journey from Guangzhou to Guilin. It was a great adventure, but we were quite startled to be sharing a very small compartment with a couple of strangers. We were all very squashed together and I didn't sleep much that night. One of the other people snored, so I lay on the top bunk looking out of the window as the Chinese countryside rushed by. We stopped in the middle of the night in, seemingly, the middle of nowhere yet hundreds of people got on and off the train. It was an incredible journey and a truly memorable trip. I used our experiences to write the story *Travelling Light*.

A few years later, I was approached to contribute to the Girls' Night In series of books by co-editing the USA and Canadian editions. This was a series of fabulous charity short story anthologies in aid of War Child. We had some amazing writers on board: Marian Keyes, Sophie Kinsella, Jenny Colgan, Cecelia Ahern, Kathy Lette. It became an international success, appearing in the bestseller lists in Australia, the UK, the USA, France and Holland. Since 2000 the books have raised over $3 million, which has gone to help children who have been affected by war and conflict.

I'm very proud of my small involvement in this project and I think that my story, *Travelling Light*, is one of my best pieces of writing and it has a very special place in my heart. I hope you like it too.

Travelling Light

The myth is that Americans don't like to travel. Yet wherever I've been in the world they seem to get there – in droves, usually. Though I hadn't quite expected to see one here, for some reason.

'Hi,' he says, looking up from his unpacking.

I just love how casual Americans are. We Brits are so much more self-conscious, reserved, uncomfortable with etiquette. Our brothers across the pond wade in affably without preamble.

'Hello.'

'How are ya?'

'Fine, thank you.' I edge into the small compartment from the corridor of the carriage.

Our train is travelling overnight from Guangzhou to Guilin and I've booked 'soft' class, which means that I get a lovely comfy bunk bed, a little bathroom shared between fifty of us at the end of the carriage and a pair of fluffy blue complimentary slippers from the railway company, whose name is spelled out in Chinese characters, so I can't tell you what it is. It also means, however, that I get to share with a complete stranger and it looks like this is him.

I'd sort of expected to be sharing with another woman, but then I might have learned by this stage of my travels that I should always expect the unexpected. My roommate is already wearing his complimentary slippers and his are pink and fluffy.

As they're intended for tiny Chinese feet, he's cut the toes out and is wearing them flip-flop style. I can't help but smile.

'Cool, right?' He holds up his peep-toes for my inspection.

'Very.'

Discordant Chinese musak plays, plinky-plonking over the intercom system, and there's no way of turning it off.

'Do you want to be on top or on bottom?' If only the other men in my life had been so direct. 'I'm easy,' he says.

'I'll take the top bunk, if that's okay.' I reason that if he's planning to murder me during the night, then at least I have a chance of hearing him clambering up to my eyrie. If I keep one of my boots handy I could whack him on the head before he has the chance to do his dastardly deed. These are the considerations of a lone female traveller in today's society.

'I'm Kane,' he says. 'Kane Freeman.'

I have to say that he doesn't look much like a murderer. He looks more like one of those surfer-dudes – if that's the correct term. We don't have many surfer-dudes in England, so I'm having to rely on glimpses of Hollywood teen movies for my terminology. Anyway, he's wearing surfer-type clothes. He's got shaggy blond hair that bears some witness to sun damage, a ridiculously golden tan, a freckly but otherwise perfect nose and clear blue eyes that, if I were up for being mesmerised, would be truly mesmerising.

'Alice.' I shake his hand formally because that's what Brits do.

He grins at me, my hand in his, as if this is somehow amusing. 'Nice to meet you, Alice.'

I suppose I should point out that I don't feel like an Alice. This was my mother's idea of a sober name for a well-behaved, studious child. She thought that by calling me Alice, I wouldn't climb trees or fall off my bicycle, tie fireworks to my brother's head or try to torture frogs. And, for a while, she was probably right. I have gone through life with a name that I don't feel suits me.

I tell none of this to my enforced companion, but then – out of the blue – he says, 'Well, Ali . . .'

I'm taken aback at the familiarisation of my name. No one calls me Ali. And I suddenly wonder why not.

' . . . shall we crack open a beer? It's going to be a hell of a long night.'

I don't normally drink. Stephen, my fiancé, doesn't like women who drink – or smoke, or wear revealing clothes, or say 'fuck' in public.

Kane wiggles a bottle of beer in my direction.

'Yes, please.' My feet are killing me and my shoulders are aching from the weight of my backpack. I need something to help. 'Beer would be nice.'

My new roommate snaps off the cap and offers it to me. 'I also have a French baguette and cheese.' His eyes flash with unspoken wickedness.

I barely stop myself from gasping. In mainland China, the rarity of these jewels shouldn't be underestimated. I have been travelling across the country here for three weeks now and have lived on nothing but noodles – prawn noodles, chicken noodles, occasionally beef noodles. Noodles, noodles, noodles and more bloody noodles. And, if it isn't noodles, then it's rice. Rice, rice, rice. Fried or boiled. It all tastes the same. Dairy products and bread are as scarce as blue diamonds. Frankly, this man could ask me to perform any dastardly deed he jolly well liked for a quick bite of his baguette.

'Oh, my word.'

He gives a smug smile, knowing that he has me in his grasp. Kane starts to prepare our impromptu picnic while I heave my rucksack onto the top bunk and fuss with settling in for the journey.

12

The small compartment is spic and span. We have a lacy tablecloth on a little shelf by the window which bears a plastic rose in a silver-coloured vase. There are lacy curtains at the window, obscuring the view of the seething mass of humanity at Guangzhou station. I have never seen anywhere as crowded in my entire life. I have never before been taller than everyone else around me. I have never before been pointed at so often as an oddity.

I inspect the bedding, which is spotless, starched within an inch of its life and embroidered with the same characters as our complimentary footwear.

Putting on my slippers, I position my boots in case I need them as a weapon and slide down to sit next to Kane on his bed. It feels terribly intimate to be in this situation with someone I've barely been introduced to. Stephen would pass out if he could see me now.

Kane carefully slices the cheese onto the bread. I can feel myself salivating and sink my teeth in gratefully the minute he hands it over. I can't help it: I groan with ecstasy. Unless you've been there, you will never imagine how good this tastes.

Kane shows off his set of perfect pearly whites. 'Good, huh?'

'Mmm. Marvellous.'

The train whistle blows and we rattle out of the station, out of the town, leaving the squash of people behind and head into the countryside.

'So,' he mutters through his bread. 'You're travelling alone?'

I like men who are keen eyed and sharp-witted. 'Yes.' It pains me to have to pause in my eating. 'I'm getting married in a few weeks.' I want him to be absolutely clear from the beginning that I'm not available. I would flash my gorgeous engagement ring – which is a whopper – but I've left it at home in case I got mugged. 'This is my last chance to travel alone.'

Kane frowns. 'Should you want to travel alone if you're getting hitched?'

He isn't the first person to voice this concern. My parents were particularly vocal. As was Stephen.

'I just needed to get away,' I say. 'It was all getting too much. I had to escape. You know how it is.'

'No,' he says. 'I've never gotten close.'

'Oh.' I give a dismissive wave of my hand. 'There are so many things to organise. It's hell.'

'So why are you doing it?'

My French bread nearly falls out of my mouth. Why *am* I doing it? 'My fiancé, Stephen, we've been together for years. Many *happy* years. He felt it was time we settled down.'

'So you're here on a Chinese train with a stranger and he's at home ordering bridal corsages?'

I give a carefree laugh. 'You make it sound a lot worse than it is.'

Kane contemplates that while he chews. 'He must be an understanding man.'

'He's very . . . understanding.' Actually, I'm not sure that Stephen understands me at all.

Kane says nothing. We eat in silence. Try as I might, I can't recapture the joy of my cheese again.

'What about you?'

Kane shrugs. 'I've always been a drifter. I like to see the world. I have no ties, no commitments, no permanent base. I go wherever the wind blows me.'

I can't even begin to imagine what that must feel like. My life is layer upon layer of commitment, confinement, duty. I live by timetables, schedules, appointments, mortgage payments. Doesn't everyone?

We finish our meal and the grinning guard comes and checks our tickets and gives us a thermos of hot water for tea.

I reciprocate for the bread and cheese by supplying tea bags. We Brits may like to travel the four corners of the globe, but we also like to do it with 'proper' tea.

'Do you work?' Kane asks as he examines his brew suspiciously. Quite frankly, most Americans just don't understand the concept of decent tea so I don't wait for his approval.

'I did. As a radio producer.' I had to resign from my job to take this trip as my employers at Let the Good Times Roll Radio also failed to 'understand' my need to fly – particularly when I've already got two weeks in the Bahamas booked as a honeymoon. Who could possibly want more than that? And yet I do. Is that greedy? Does it make me a bad person? 'I'm taking some time out.' Not necessarily voluntarily. 'I'll look for something else when all the fuss from the wedding has died down.'

'You're using a lot of negative images with reference to your forthcoming nuptials,' Kane observes.

'That sounds terribly Californian, if you don't mind me saying,' I observe back.

He smiles. 'I am from California. I'm allowed.'

At ten o'clock it's lights out on Chinese trains, which reminds me of my time at boarding school. The sudden plunge into darkness curtails our conversation and we scrabble to our bunks, clicking on the faint night lights above our heads. I decide to stay clothed for modesty's sake, but Kane has no such inhibitions. He's wearing battered, baggy shorts and a sleeveless T-shirt that bears the faded remains of a logo, now too pale to discern. I'm used to a man who favours pressed chinos and striped shirts and who goes into the bathroom to change. In a moment, Kane is stripped down to his boxer shorts. He's clearly comfortable with his body and I suspect if I had a body like that, I would be too. I know that I should look away, but I'm afraid to say, I can't. I just can't. He has a tattoo of a dragon high on the

15

broad sweep of his shoulder. I wonder where he had it done and if it hurt him and I find myself thinking that I'd like to trace the outline with my finger.

He turns and smiles up at me. I do hope he's not a mind reader. 'Sleep tight,' he says and hops into the bunk below me.

I do no such thing. I lie awake looking at the air vent in the ceiling, occasionally peeping out of the lace curtain to the blackness of the paddy fields beyond and watching as, even through the dark hours, we stop at brightly-lit stations to let hundreds of passengers come and go.

The train runs minute-perfect. Stephen would like that part of it. Stephen likes things to be regular. His habits, his meals, his bowels. Sorry, that's not nice of me. You don't need to know that. Even though it's true.

Stephen, on the other hand, wouldn't like the crowds, the smells, the squatty loos – apologies, back to toilet preferences again – the food, the heat, the pollution, the whole damn foreignness of the place. We'll be taking our holidays in the Caribbean from now on with maybe the odd deviation to the Cote d'Azur. We'll stay in five-star hotels, with fluffy towels and spa facilities – someplace where we don't have to mix too closely with the locals. We won't even have to trouble ourselves to go to the bar for a drink, it'll be brought to us on a tray at our sun-loungers by a smiling waiter. Is this what I want?

I close my eyes and try not to think of anything connected with the wedding. Have you ever felt like everything was crowding in on you? My whole world was becoming smaller and smaller, until I felt like my namesake, Alice in Wonderland, after she'd drunk the potion and had shrunk to barely ten inches high. I felt I just didn't matter any more, that I had become too tiny to be of consequence. My days were taken up with invitations and flowers and bell-ringers and wedding cars and who the hell was I going to sit next to who? Everyone gets pre-wedding nerves, I was told – time after time. Is that all it is, this nagging feeling? I screw my eyes tighter shut but still sleep eludes me. The stations, towns, miles flash by. I hear the sound of my neighbour's soft snoring from the bunk below. Kane doesn't look like the sort of man who worries if he misses a poo.

Bang on time, the train pulls into Guilin station just after dawn. Kane and I haven't said much to each other this morning. Kane, because he's only just woken up after sleeping like a bear – his words, not mine. Me, because I'm not sure what I want to say.

We pack our rucksacks, bumping into each other in the tiny space as we prepare to leave the train. The doors open and the slow shuffle towards the exit starts. Kane and I make to join it.

'Thanks for the bread and cheese,' I say. 'It's been nice . . .'

'Where are you heading for?' Kane asks.

'Yangshuo.'

'I've been there before,' he informs me. 'It's a blast. I know a great hotel. Want to hang out together?'

I nod, mainly because my brain is urging my mouth to say no.

The Fawlty Towers hotel in Yangshuo is, indeed a great place. It has showers complete with hot water and clean sheets. And 'hanging out together' also seems to involve sharing a room. Single beds – I'm not that reckless. After spending a night together it seemed churlish to refuse and it will help keep down the costs. I don't think I'll mention it to Stephen though. It's another thing he wouldn't understand.

Kane rents bicycles with dodgy brakes and we head out into the countryside, weaving our way through narrow valleys and straggly villages whose houses are still pasted with red and gold new year banners to bring good luck to those inside. Weather-worn mountains moulded by the rain into sugarloaf

17

shapes tower over us. I can't remember when I was last on a bike and I'd forgotten how great the wind in your hair feels as it lifts the strands away from your neck to kiss the humid dampness away. We climb Moon Hill, Kane tugging me up the steep slope by the hand, until we look over the landscape that spawned a thousand paintings – soft, misty mountains, meandering rivers, the pink blush of cherry blossom trees. I return to Yangshuo feeling achy and strangely liberated – like a dog who's dared to stick its head out of a car window for the first time.

In the Hard Luck Internet Café, I pick up an email from Stephen.

Hello Alice – the caterers have suggested these canapés. There is a list of a dozen nibbly-bits, all of which sound perfectly acceptable. *Shall I give them the go ahead? Stephen.*

I stare at a picture of Bruce Lee on the wall and wonder if you should be addressing your future wife 'Hello Alice' – particularly when she's been away for nearly three weeks. Shouldn't the word 'love' appear in there somewhere? Perhaps Stephen is beginning to wonder why his future wife *has* been away for nearly three weeks. There has been a distinct lack of 'I'm missing you' type emails. But then Stephen is very reserved with his emotions. It's one of the things I love about him. Really, it is. I've never been one for gushy stuff.

I type: *Dear Stephen. Canapés sound fine.* And then in a rush of guilt or something: *Missing you. Love Alice.*

As I head back to the hotel, I see Kane sitting outside the Planet China restaurant drinking green tea and Yanjing beer with his feet up on a chair. I've never seen anyone look so laid back. My stomach lurches when I approach him and it might not be due to the fact I'm back on the noodle diet. How old is Kane, I wonder? The same as me? Not quite thirty. He is so loose and carefree with his life that it makes me feel older than time itself. I plonk myself down next to him and hear myself sigh wearily.

'You look stressed.'

'I am.'

'Wedding arrangements not going to plan?' Kane grins. I'm sure he doesn't believe that this wedding is ever going to go ahead.

'I've just agreed the canapés,' I say crisply. 'They're going to be wonderful.'

'Try this.' He hands me a cigarette.

'I didn't know you smoked.' But then there's a lot I don't know about Kane, even though I'm sharing a hotel room with him. I have no idea why I'm taking this as I don't smoke either. Stephen doesn't like women who . . . oh, you get the gist.

'It's herbal,' he says. 'It will relax you.'

I drag deeply on the cigarette and then the smell hits me. 'Oh good grief,' I say. 'Do you know what this is?'

Kane grins at me.

'Of course you do.' I take another tentative puff. I'm not a natural law-breaker. 'Is this legal here?' I suspect not. It's making me even less relaxed than I was. I can't do drugs, not even soft ones. Quickly, I hand it back. 'I could end up in prison for twenty-five years.'

Kane fixes me with a wily stare. 'Isn't that where you're headed anyway?'

'I need a drink.'

In what sounds to me like passable Mandarin, Kane orders me a steaming glass of jasmine tea and some rough Chinese vodka. I pick my way through the beautiful white blooms, inhaling the fragrance as I sip the tea, spoiling it with the raw cut of the alcohol as I chase it with swigs of vodka. I was going to have jasmine in my wedding bouquet, but now it will always remind me of Kane. And that might not be a good thing.

19

From Yangshuo we take a plane to Chengdu to see the giant pandas and I don't want you to read too much into this, but we're already acting like an old married couple. I can't believe how easily I've fallen into step with this man. At the airport Kane looks after the passports while I go and top up on 'western' snacks – potato chips and boiled sweets rather than scorpions on sticks.

The next morning, we join the old grannies in the park doing tai chi, causing great hilarity as we heave our bulky frames alongside the delicate, bird-like movements of the elderly Chinese ladies. Kane causes a particular stir. He laughs as they cluck round him like mother hens and come to touch his spiky blond hair and his bulging biceps, which makes me flush as it's something I've considered doing myself. The old men, some in ageing Maoist uniforms, promenade proudly with their songbirds in cages and a feeling of sadness and oppression settles over me. Without speaking Kane takes my hand and squeezes. I can feel the edge of my engagement ring cutting into my finger even though I'm not wearing it, but I don't try to pull away.

Kane keeps holding my hand while we travel further into the country to visit the Terracotta Army at Xian. Beautiful, untouchable soldiers, frozen in time, unable to move forward. I cry at the sheer spectacle of it and at other things that I can't even begin to voice. He's still holding my hand a week later when we hike up to the mist-shrouded peak of Emei Shan and book a simple room in the extraordinary peace of a Buddhist monastery that looks like something out of a film set.

We have dinner in a local café with no windows and a tarpaulin roof, lit only by smoky kerosene lamps, the sound of monkeys chattering in the trees high above us. A group of local men play mah-jong boisterously in the corner, each tile slapped down with a challenge and hotly contested. A scraggy cat sits hopefully at my feet. We're the only diners and the waif-like

Chinese owner brings us dish after dish of succulent, stir-fried vegetables: aubergine, spring greens, bean sprouts, water chestnuts.

Kane has been on the internet at the monastery. It makes you realise that there's nowhere in the world that can truly be classed as remote any more. It also makes me realise that our time together is coming to an end. He's planning another leg of this trip which will eventually take him round the world. I had always dreamed of travelling the world and I feel a pang of envy that he'll be continuing the rest of his journey without me. He says the surf is good in Australia right now and that he'll probably head out that way. See? I knew my assessment of him was right all along. Do surfers attract groupies? I think they do. And I wonder will he hook up with someone else as easy? Someone less tied, less uptight, less duty-bound.

Kane is adept with his chopsticks while I still handle them like knitting needles. Give me a plate of chow mein and I could run you up a sweater, no problem. We finish our meal and bask in the warm night air with cups of jasmine tea. He plucks at the plaited friendship bracelet on his wrist and not for the first time, I contemplate when and how he acquired it. We both look so terribly mellow in this half-light and I wish I could capture this moment forever. Me and Kane cocooned in our own microcosm.

His fingers wander across the table and find mine. 'Just in case you were wondering,' he says gently. 'This brother–sister thing we're doing is taking its toll on me.'

I don't know what to say, so I say nothing.

Kane sighs, his eyes searching mine. 'What I really want is to make love to you.'

'Oh,' I say. 'Okay.'

He looks at me for confirmation and I nod. 'Let's go.'

Kane wraps his arms around me and holds me tightly as we pay the bill and hurry back to the shelter of the monastery. Is

21

it a sin to make love in a monastery? I don't know. I don't want to know. I'm too Catholic by half. I might burn in hell for this at some later stage, but I think it will be worth it. Can something so beautiful be punishable by fire and brimstone? I hope the monks don't mind. I wouldn't like to offend anyone. As I hold onto Kane in the dark, I don't consider that it might be a sin against Stephen. I don't consider anything but the curve of Kane's spine, the strength of his arms and the look of love on his face. And it takes me by surprise, as no one has looked at me with such passion for a long, long time.

We take another overnight train to Beijing, to the Forbidden City. How appropriate. This time we squeeze together in one bunk, making love to the rhythm of the rattling rails, falling asleep in each other's arms.

The pollution in Beijing is worse in the Spring, when the sands from the Gobi desert blend with the exhaust fumes of a million, ozone-unfriendly cars. The mixture stings your eyes, strips your throat and makes it hard to see too far ahead. A grey veil blocks out the sun which tries hard to break through, but is generally thwarted.

When in China you must do as the Chinese do and we hire sit-up-and-beg bikes again to cycle through the jammed streets to the vast expanse of Tiananmen Square – the symbol of freedom to an oppressed world. We join the throng of Chinese tourists flying kites and are royally ripped off as we buy flimsy paper butterflies from a canny, bow-legged vendor. He could feed his family for a week on what we pay him for a moment's fleeting pleasure, but I begrudge him nothing as our lives are so easy compared to his. It makes me appreciate that I have very little to complain about.

We laugh as we run through the square, trailing our kites behind us, watching them as they duck and dive, playing with the erratic wind. But even then, I notice that my kite is not as exuberant in its swoops and soars as Kane's. It's more hesitant, fearful and it's tearing easily. I trail after him while he takes the lead, clearing a route through the crowd, leaving me to follow behind. And then he holds me close and I forget everything. I forget to hold tightly to my kite and it floats away, bobbing, bobbing on the air, reaching for the hidden sun until it's quite out of sight. Free.

'I love you,' Kane says. But I watch my kite fly away from me.

Email from Stephen. *Hello Alice – have ordered cars. Think you'll like them. Doctor and Mrs Smythe have said no. Shame. Missing you too. Stephen.*

Is it a shame that two people who I don't even know aren't coming to my wedding? Do I really care what car will take me there? I stare at the screen, but can't make my fingers type a reply. Now what do I do?

That night Kane and I lie on the bed in our horrible Western-style hotel which has matching bedspreads and curtains and shower gel and shampoo in tiny identical bottles. Already I can feel my other life calling me.

'Have you told him?' Kane asks.

'No,' I say.

'You can't go back,' my lover states. 'You know you can't.'

But I can. And I will. I can't explain this to Kane, but I love Stephen because he's anchored in reality. He understands about pensions, for heaven's sake. He polishes his shoes. He has chosen the wedding limousines. He may not make love to me as if it is the last thing he will ever do in this life. He may not chase life with an insatiable, unquenchable thirst. But Stephen is safe and solid and secure. We'll grow old together. We'll have a joint bank account. I will never feel the same about anyone in my entire life as I do about Kane – never. Not even Stephen. Kane is the sun, the moon and the stars. He is all the things I'm not, but that I would want to be. In a different life. I have never loved anyone more or as hopelessly. But Kane is as flighty as the paper butterfly kites, answering every tug of the breeze. How can you base a future, a whole lifetime, on something as unreliable as that? What would we do? Spend our lives wandering the earth, hand-in-hand, rucksack slung on back. Or would there come a time when I'd want to settle down, to pin the butterfly to the earth, stamp on it, crush it flat? Would I eventually become Kane's Stephen?

We make love and, this time, I feel that it *is* the last thing that I will ever do in my life. Every nerve, fibre, tissue, cell of my body zings with the prospect of life. Beneath him I lose myself, my reason, my mind. I'm part of Kane and he'll always be a part of me. But this excitement would die, wouldn't it? Could we always maintain this intensity, this intimacy? Isn't it better to have loved so hard and so briefly than to watch it sink and vanish from view like the setting sun?

I wake up and reach for Kane, but he's gone. The bed beside me is empty. There's nothing left of my lover but a crumpled imprint in the sheets. I pad to the bathroom and take a shower, concentrating on the chipped tiles so that I won't feel that my heart is having to force itself to keep beating. You can taste devastation – did you know that? I didn't until now. It coats your teeth, tongue and throat and no amount of spearmint mouthwash will get rid of it.

I decide to check out of the hotel, even though my homeward flight isn't until tomorrow. I can't stay here alone. Not now. Slowly, methodically, I pack up my things and take the lift down to reception where I queue for an interminable amount of time behind a party of jocular Americans to pay my bill. I told you. They get everywhere. Inside your undies, inside your heart, inside your soul. Eventually, I reach the desk and hand over my credit card and my key. In return I get a receipt and a business card. The receptionist taps it.

'It was left for you,' he says.

I flip it over and my broken heart flips too. Somehow its jagged edges mesh back together. There's a caricature of a scruffy surfer and in big, bold type: *Barney's Surf Shack, Bondi Beach.* Kane has scribbled. *I'll wait there every day for two weeks.*

But I don't think he'll need to. I know now that there'll be no wedding. No hymns. No white dress. No bridesmaids. Not now. And maybe not ever. Yet I know that it's the right thing to do. I only hope that Stephen will understand. He deserves more. I shouldn't spend my life with someone I can live with. I should be with someone I can't live without. Wherever that may take me. My pension fund will just have to wait.

I hail a taxi and jump inside. I might just make it.

'Beijing Airport!' I say. 'As quick as you can!' My word, I've always wanted to say that! It doesn't matter that the driver can't even speak English. He must sense my haste as he careens out in to the six lanes of traffic, horn blaring. I feel as if I'm swimming in champagne, bubbles rising inside of me.

We pull up outside the terminal building and I race inside. There standing by the check-in desk is an unmistakable figure. His rucksack is over his shoulder. He's head and shoulders above everyone else. One blond mop above a sea of black.

I run towards him as fast as I can. 'Kane!'

He turns. And when he sees me he smiles.

I love Venice. It's one of my favourite cities. Some years ago Lovely Kev and I were fortunate enough to travel across Italy by train and our first few days were spent in Venice. The first day it was glorious sunshine, the temperature soared and the sun sparkled on the Grand Canal. The next day couldn't have been more different. Rain poured down all day. The Grand Canal turned grey and surly. Water gushed from the gargoyles on the basilica and St Mark's square flooded. It was impossible to go anywhere and we spent a good deal of the day in restaurants drinking creamy cappuccinos and red wine, reading our books and eating pizza. It was fabulous and I think I loved it more than in the sunshine.

When I first started writing I joined the Romantic Novelists' Association and they have been a tremendous source of support and encouragement over the years. I've met so many lovely and like-minded friends in what is, generally, quite a solitary occupation. Many of the members also seem to appreciate the restorative properties of sparkly drinks too!

When they put together their first short story anthology, Loves Me, Loves Me Not, I was invited to contribute and was delighted to oblige. My time in Venice seemed to be the perfect setting for a story.

A Weekend in Venice

It was already spitting when I left the hotel after an uninspiring breakfast of dry white bread and tasteless rubbery cheese. Now the rain is steady, settled in, not planning on blowing over in a pesky squall. This downpour is shaping up to give us a bad-tempered and thorough soaking and I think the bread at breakfast might be the only dry thing I see all day. The sky is low-slung, draped heavily over the tops of the ornate buildings. Venice in September, I hoped, would be full of sun, full of fun. Instead, it's full of tourists and full of water.

Winding my way through the maze of narrow backstreets, cobbles slick with rain, I make my way to St Mark's Square to find my tour guide. She's already in full flow, speaking to a huge group of Japanese tourists, by the time I arrive. The guide is older than me, maybe ten years, but she's unutterably stylish – the sort of chic that older Italian women do so well. There's a red silk scarf tied jauntily round the hips of her tight black jeans and she's carrying a matching red umbrella which she hasn't put up despite the rain. Instead, she stands under the shelter of the arches around the damp façade of the Doges Palace while her tour group listen patiently in the pouring rain. My Japanese companions may be untroubled by this, clothed as they are in bright yellow rain capes and matching hats and shod in makeshift, tie-on Wellingtons that are being sold on the corner of every sodden street. I, in my summer-weight pea coat from Monsoon (how appropriate) and heeled suede boots, am less so.

The guide, Silvana, drones on for far too long about the historical importance of Venice as a trade route while the Japanese nod vigorously and we all get very wet. My attention drifts and I stare out into St Mark's Square. The place is unusually empty, all the outdoor cafés closed up, battened down, chairs stacked. Even the droves of street-wise pigeons have gone into hiding.

I should have been in Venice with Jerrard. The weekend trip was booked to mark our fifth anniversary together. We met at a work-related conference on The Ethics of Green Marketing, which always seemed such a terribly dull place a start to a love affair. To counteract this, we always went somewhere extravagantly romantic to celebrate the ticking off of another year together. Except this year, we didn't make it. This year Jerrard felt that our relationship wasn't going anywhere. He felt 'the whole thing' had become stale. He felt we should spend some time apart. *I* felt that meant he found someone younger and more obliging. Someone who didn't nag him about leaving the remnants of his beard in the bathroom sink after he'd shaved or didn't make him pull his weight with the household chores. If he had met someone else, he wouldn't say. Jerrard felt unable to share that information with me. But he moved out, anyway.

I couldn't bear to see the weekend go to waste – call me frugal. As Jerrard did on many occasions. It was bought and paid for. If I had been Jerrard, I would have gone to Venice anyway, hoping that it might reignite the spark that had been long missing. If that spark had still remained elusive, *then* I'd have called a halt. There's an etiquette to these things that he failed to understand.

He was unmoved by my begging. Take someone else, he urged. A salve to his own conscience, perhaps. I didn't want to come with someone else. I wanted to be here with Jerrard. I wanted him to have a last-minute change of heart. I wanted him to call me at the eleventh hour and then sigh with relief when I told him, that no, no one else had taken his place. No one else *could* take his place.

Of course, he didn't call. I've heard precious little from him. He walked out of my life without looking back to see if I was OK, if I would survive without him, if I was still in love with him.

I am.

Inside the Doges Palace, we trail around after the fragrant Silvana, moving through the crush of wet, doggy-smelling people, trying to admire the dark beauty of the Tintorettos while outside the rain gets heavier and heavier. My attention wanders to the window. Outside, great plumes of water spray from the mouths of the grimacing Gargoyles on all corners of the roof, showering into courtyard below, and it's easy to see why Venice is slowly being consumed by the rising tides.

The next part of our tour is supposed to be St Mark's famous Basilica. As I splash through ankle-deep puddles, thoroughly ruining my favourite boots, Silvana tells us with an insouciant shrug that the church is closed due to flooding. A high wind shouldering the waves across the lagoon has added its power to the rain and our tour is to be curtailed.

I booked the tour because I didn't want to mooch around Venice alone and lonely. Being in a group, I thought, would give my emotions the shelter they required. It's not to be. Anyway, to be honest, the incessant chatter and the clicking of camera shutters were not exactly enhancing my Venice Experience.

As the rest of the group all move away, I decide to seek solace in a restaurant. A glass of good Rioja, some tiramisu and maybe a hot, frothy cappuccino will surely restore my flagging spirits. Empty gondolas are tied up at the moorings, black, mournful,

29

bobbing angrily at their enforced idleness. Their po-faced gondoliers are holed up in neighbouring cafés, conspicuous in their striped jerseys and comic boaters thinking of all the tourists they've failed to ensnare, all the euros that haven't changed hands, how many times 'O Sole Mio' hasn't been crooned. Today, Venice has pulled down its designer-labelled trousers and has bared its bottom at the tourists.

Cowering beneath my ineffectual umbrella, my long blonde hair plastered flat to my head, I find a pizzeria with steamed-up windows and a cheerful hum of conversation inside. I think I'm lucky to score the last table, until I find I'm sitting next to two American couples who talk in loud voices about how they're 'doing Europe'. Today is Monday, so it must be Italy. Tuesday is France. Wednesday, England. My pizza is soggy, my wine is sharp, my tiramisu synthetic, my coffee and the service both lukewarm. The urge to phone Jerrard and cry is almost unbearable. Thank goodness the wine is awful, otherwise I might be tempted to down a whole bottle.

When I can linger no longer over an empty cup, I tip the waiter badly as a small revenge for his indifference and head out into the downpour once more. The weather doesn't seem to be deterring the crowds and I squeeze my way towards the Rialto Bridge and the sanctuary of my hotel. On my bedside table, there's a good book – a cheesy romance, but right now I need a happy ending. I'll have a hot bath, chill out, try not to think about what Jerrard's doing now and read about the tangled love lives of others.

The steady stream of tourists thins out to a trickle as I take the lesser-used backstreets to my hotel. The rain is worse, my umbrella less than useless. I look up, dodging the drips from my umbrella's spokes, and don't recognise my surroundings. Somewhere in my haste, huddled down, I've missed my turning. I should have taken the street with a little shop on the corner, its window is filled with carnival masques in red, black and silver – exotic, opulent, erotic. Each time I've passed I've stopped to drool over them, but their prices are way beyond my meagre budget. Now I can't see it anywhere. I'm in a similar courtyard by a metal bridge, but not the right one and I don't know which way to go. My feet are cold, numb with pain. My map, like my romantic novel, is on my bedside table. I decide that I hate this city. The rain is too heavy, the people too grumpy, the canals too smelly, the prices too extortionate, the pigeons too many, the pasta too fattening, the tourists too stupid. Tears run down my face. I'm alone and lost in Venice and I don't know what to do.

When I've done enough self-pitying snivelling, I look up and try to get my bearings. *Come on, Beth, get a grip*, I chide. *You're a little bit lost, nothing more.*

Across the courtyard, there's a smart house. Its front door is bright red as are its balconies – surreal highlights in an otherwise monochrome scene. A small motor boat bobs by the door, next to a chalkboard which has a phrase scrawled on it in a variety of different languages. The lettering is rapidly disappearing as fat drips of rain run down it. I can just about pick out the English version. MODELS REQUIRED, it says.

The door is ajar. Perhaps someone in there can tell me the way to my hotel. Before I can think better of it, I fold my umbrella, push open the door and go inside. The hall is dimly lit, but warm and only serves to make me realise how cold I am. I shiver and call out, 'Hello.' My heels click on the caramel-coloured, Venetian marble floor, echoing through the hall. 'Hello?'

A door opens ahead of me and a tall man stands in the frame. The room behind him is light and airy, so I can't see his face. He says, 'You've come for the modelling?'

'No, no,' I answer. 'I'm lost. I'm looking for the Hotel Segusa.'

31

'Ah,' he says. 'Then you are very lost.'

'It's the rain.' I shrug as if it's an explanation. Nothing to do with my inability to remember to carry my map, of course.

'You are very wet,' he remarks. 'And you look cold.'

'I'm both,' I agree.

'Then come into my studio. Sit down. Wait. The rain will stop.'

'I don't want to disturb your work.'

'I am not working,' he says. 'I have no model. No muse. I am playing.'

It's tempting. My curiosity is piqued and the ancient radiator churning out heat is very appealing.

He opens the door wider, lights floods over him. His hair is dark and curling. His body is long, lean, athletic. A black T-shirt and jeans cling tightly to him, outlining his muscles and his slim hips. His skin is olive, a native, and when he smiles the room lights up some more. 'Come.' He beckons me with slender, artistic fingers.

Hesitant, I follow him into the studio. The room is bright white, the roof is made of glass and looks tear-stained with the rivulets of rain. There's a huge black leather couch and a large easel standing at one end. Behind the easel is another enormous window with a view over the bleak, slate-grey canal. A table filled with paints stands next to the easel.

'Oh,' I say. 'You're an artist.'

He laughs.

'I mean, well, you don't look like an artist.' He doesn't exactly comply with the typical image of starving artist in a grotty garret. I thought he was a photographer, that kind of studio.

'I don't know what an artist is supposed to look like.' His Italian accent is tinged with an American twang and I wonder if he's spent some time overseas. 'I'm Marcello.'

He holds out his hand and I take it. 'Beth,' I reciprocate.

32

'I have coffee, Beth. Would you like some?'

'Please.'

There's a small kitchen area at the far end of the studio and Marcello goes to busy himself with making coffee while I stand and drip self-consciously on his floor.

'Take off your things,' he says to me. 'Be more comfortable.'

If only I could. I look round for something to do with my umbrella.

'Let me.' Marcello comes back with two cups of coffee which he puts on the table with his paints. 'Your umbrella.'

I hand it over.

'Now your jacket.' I peel the wet sleeves away from my arms. Beneath it my T-shirt is soaked.

Marcello tsks at me. 'A cold will take you to your death. Off, off. I will find you a shirt.'

'But . . . I . . .'

'I work with naked women every day,' he says with a casual shrug. 'I am not shy.'

But I am. Before I can voice that particular thought, he's off, dumping my umbrella in the kitchen, hanging my coat over the back of a chair.

I have goosepimples on my arms and probably over the rest of my body. To distract me from my current predicament, I take in the artworks on the walls. There are, indeed, a lot of naked women, beautifully displayed, open, wanting, sensual.

Marcello returns and tosses a shirt at me. It's warm, dry. He shrugs again. 'What else are you going to do this afternoon? Take off all of your clothes. When you are warm again and we have drunk our coffee, I will paint you.'

My arms fold across my chest in an involuntary movement. 'I don't think . . .'

'You must not think at all,' he instructs. 'You must just do it.' Then he gives me my coffee cup.

Maybe Marcello has drugged me, because as soon as I finish my coffee I'm so terribly tired, my limbs are heavy, leaden and I don't have the wherewithal to want to move. But, frankly, I don't care what he's done to me. Even though he's a stranger, I somehow feel safe here, sheltered in a warm cocoon. Maybe it's just relief that someone has taken control. My eyelids feel heavy. The rain clearly has no intention of easing up. It pours in torrents down the windows, drumming rhythmically, cutting us off from the world. He's left the room and my clothes are uncomfortably damp, so, tentatively, I tug my T-shirt over my head. With my back to the door, I hurriedly unhook my bra and slip on his shirt. It's warm and soft, comforting, on my chilled skin.

I pull off my boots. They're ruined, wet through, but, at the moment, I don't care. Wriggling my jeans over my hips, I'm relieved to see that the shirt falls to mid-thigh and covers me with reasonable modesty.

'Sit down,' Marcello says when he comes back. 'Just relax.'

I edge onto the black sofa, curl my legs under me and try to look casual. He laughs at my discomfort. 'Pretend I am not here.'

How can I when he's staring at me so intently? I let my head fall back against a pillow. He goes to stand behind his easel. Then the reality of the situation hits me and I sit up straight again. 'I can't do this,' I tell him. 'Really. I'm far too straight-laced.'

Marcello smiles at me. 'I don't know what straight-laced is, but it sounds very nice to me.'

'I must go.'

'Wait,' he says. 'Now that you're here, I cannot let you go.'

A thrill of panic runs through me. He holds out a hand. 'Don't move. Don't move. I will make it all better.'

He reaches behind him and draws out a carnival masque

from under a black sheet. I gasp when I see it. The eyepiece is feline, covered with rich red velvet the colour of a Venetian whore's lips. It's thickly encrusted with sequins and ruby-red jewels. Above it, plumes of feathers stand proud, ruffling of their own volition. It's menacing, marvellous. Exciting and erotic.

'That's fabulous.'

His smile is indulgent. 'I knew you would like it.'

I wonder has it been worn before, maybe by some glamorous woman dancing and posing her way through the streets of Venice, entertaining the crowd.

Marcello hands it to me. 'Put it on.'

'I can't.'

He looks bemused. 'Why not?'

It looks too mysterious, too daring and I'm strangely nervous of its allure. I'm not sure that I'm worthy of it. 'I don't know.'

'It will suit you,' Marcello assures me.

So, I brush back my damp hair and put it on. It fits perfectly, moulding to the contours of my cheeks, the bridge of my nose. The weight of it is reassuring. I look at him through the slits of the eyes and the masque makes me feel like a different person entirely.

'Get on the couch.'

Much to my own astonishment, I obey. Marcello arranges black pillows around my shoulders.

'Take off that shirt.' From nowhere, Marcello produces a sheath of blood-red crushed velvet. 'Drape this over you.'

I strip off the shirt and do as instructed, covering my breasts with the fabric.

'Leave them bare,' Marcello says. 'I want to see them.'

Laying back on the sofa, my head rests on the pillows. I let the fabric fall to my waist.

'Pull it high,' he says. 'High on your legs. Your thighs are magnificent.'

I don't think anyone has ever told me that before. My hands inch the velvet higher.

'Great,' Marcello murmurs. 'Wonderful.' He picks up a paint brush. 'You look beautiful. *Bella, bellisimo*. Think amazing thoughts.'

I lay back on the pillows, breasts and thighs bared, arms lifted above my head, and wonder what Jerrard would say if he could see me now.

'The light is gone. I can paint you no more,' Marcello says as he puts down his brush. 'I can only remember you with the light of my eye.'

I'm tired, woozy; the hours have gone by while I've lain here, my mind in happy freefall. I go to sit up. 'I must go.'

'No.' Marcello comes to sit by me. 'First I must love you,' he tells me. 'Then I must feed you.'

He laughs at the surprise on my face. Then he shrugs. 'It is the Italian way.'

Taking the soft velvet in his hands, he caress my breasts with it, making my back arch. He strips off his clothes, effortlessly, as he covers me with kisses, murmuring, murmuring '*bella, bella*' as he does. Then, when he is naked and above me, he takes the strip of velvet and binds my wrists together as he holds my arms above my head. I want all of him inside me. More, more, more.

Then we twist together and I straddle him. I unbind my wrists and slip the velvet over his eyes, tying the blindfold behind his head while my tongue travels his body. The feathers on my masque shiver with excitement and the feeling travels through my body, ripples tensing and thrilling until I throw my head back and moan with pleasure.

For a long time we lie together, Marcello's arms around me. The drumming of the rain has finally stopped. The silence is comfortable and welcome. Then Marcello says, 'And now, I promised I would feed you. I must do so.'

He eases away from me and pads, still naked, to the kitchen. I lie and stare at the ceiling, spent, exhausted, exhilarated, not knowing what to think. When Marcello comes back, he brings a platter with bread, cheese, Parma ham and figs. Then he brings a bottle of wine and glasses.

Somewhat reluctantly, I sit up and take off the masque. 'I feel like another woman in this.'

'No.' He takes my hand. 'I think you feel more like yourself.'

We curl against each other as we eat. I'm ravenous. It's like I haven't eaten properly for years. The cheese is rich and smoked, the bread fresh, crunchy; the ham, salty on my tongue like Marcello. He drizzles red wine from his fingers over my breasts and laps it with his hot tongue. The juice of the figs runs down my chin and I giggle as he kisses it away.

'Can I see the painting?'

'No,' he says. 'Not yet.'

'But when? I leave tomorrow.'

'You will know.'

'How?'

'Be patient.' He puts a finger to my lips and doesn't say any more.

When we've finished the food and drunk our fill of the wine, I get dressed. My clothes are still damp. I pull on my jeans and, after the warmth of the studio, they feel deeply unpleasant against my skin.

'Keep the shirt,' Marcello says.

I can smell the scent of his body on it. I try very hard to catch a peek of the painting, just a tiny glimpse, but my artist is having none of it. He steers me away to the other side of the studio.

'Well,' I say, when I'm fully attired once more and have my soggy umbrella to hand, 'that was a very interesting afternoon.' Much better than some fusty old church.

'Take this too.' He gives me the carnival masque.

'No. No,' I say. 'This must have cost a fortune.'

'Take it,' he insists. 'It will always remind you of the time we have spent together.'

'I'd like that.' I give him a peck on the cheek as I clutch the carnival masque to me.

'Give me your telephone number.'

I scribble it on the piece of paper that Marcello offers. 'Now you'd better tell me how to get back to my hotel.'

At the cherry-red front door, Marcello gives me meticulous directions. I kiss him goodbye. This time, a long, lingering kiss. My fingers trace the contours of his face, committing them to memory. 'Thank you.'

'It was my pleasure.' We kiss again and he runs his fingers through my hair. 'I would like to spend more time with you, *bella* Beth,' he says, 'but I have things I must do.'

'That's fine,' I say. 'I understand.'

Then I leave. The night is cool and fresh. My steps are brisk on the slippery streets, light and carefree. I'm heading back towards my hotel, glad that I'm no longer lost.

The next day the sun is full and high in the sky. I take my breakfast by the open windows of a Juliet balcony and watch the diamonds of sunlight glitter on the surface of the Grand Canal. In my dark, shuttered room, I slept like a log, alone in my double bed – a deep sleep filled with colourful dreams of the carnival. In full carnival regalia I was parading through the streets, all eyes on me wearing my wonderful masque, low-cut dress with bustle and silk slippers on my feet, Marcello in black velvet, his hand held tightly in mine. I awoke refreshed, light in spirit and smiled at the masque propped up against the alarm clock on my beside table.

Now I'm anxious to greet the day. And what a day it is. The gondoliers are back out in force, their songs ringing out across the water. The tourists are already thronging towards the Rialto bridge. I finish my breakfast – fresh, warm bread this morning – and head back to my room.

Carefully folding Marcello's shirt, I slip it into a plastic bag that I find in the bottom of my case. This time, as well as my umbrella, I take my map and set out. My destination is Marcello's studio. My excuse, I have his shirt to return.

The going is slow – the tourists move at a snail's pace, shoulder to shoulder, through the ribbons of streets and over the tiny arched bridges, stopping to gawp in the shop windows at the masques, the jewels, the handmade paper and quill pens. I break my journey only to buy some chocolate-covered nougat, *torrone classico*, from a gorgeous chocolate shop whose tempting displays make my mouth salivate.

Retracing my steps from yesterday, I eventually find myself in the small square by Marcello's studio. Today, there's no chalk board outside and the cherry-red door is firmly closed. The bobbing boat is gone. A cold dampness encircles my heart despite the increasing heat of the day. Without hope, I knock boldly at the door and am greeted by silence. I wait patiently and knock again. Wherever Marcello is, he clearly isn't here.

Folding the plastic bag containing his shirt as small as I can, I leave it tucked down beside the door, hoping that Marcello finds it still here on his return. I want to keep the shirt to remember the scent of him but that seems too pathetic, too sad. I don't know what I'd wanted in coming back to his studio. Perhaps I wanted to check that it really did happen. Or did I think that we could have had another wonderful day together? Yes, I confess, I did. But it was as much of a dream as my glorious vision of the carnival was in my sleep. Perhaps Marcello will call me one day. But, somehow, I doubt it.

So, now I have the day to myself. I let the crowd carry me along, aimlessly, and eventually we burst out into St Mark's

Square. Today it is full of pigeons, full of tourists, full of couples holding hands. Blowing my budget, I sit outside Caffè Florian sipping a chilled Bellini and listen to the soaring strains of the tail-coated violinists, the sun bronzing my face. I eat a piece of my *torrone* to give me a sugar rush, to give my spirit a lift.

In the square a mime artist poses for the Japanese tourists, who never, ever tire of taking photographs. She's dressed in a cheap, hastily put-together carnival costume and a flimsy masque that is nothing compared to the beauty of mine. I smile contentedly. I'm not going to let the fact that Marcello isn't going to feature in my plans spoil my last day in this city. I have churches to see, paintings to marvel over, many paninis to eat. Tonight, I fly back to London and have wonderful memories to take with me and an exotic carnival masque as a souvenir to cherish.

Back at work the relentless push towards Christmas is turning us all into mad things. I have endless marketing proposals to finish, tight deadlines, even tighter budgets. My weekend in Venice seems a long time ago, Marcello a distant and wonderful memory. Any beneficial effects dissipated just as soon as I'd returned to the daily grind. Only the rich, ruby-red carnival masque smiling enigmatically at me from my bedroom wall reminds me that it ever happened at all.

Every night I go home late, exhausted, flop in front of the television and watch *I'm a Celebrity Get Me Out of Here* as I enjoy the delights of a microwaved meal on my lap and a large glass of anything remotely alcoholic.

I moved out of the flat that I rented with Jerrard into somewhere smaller, less salubrious and more affordable. Switching on the television in my cramped living room, I settle down to my night of wild entertainment. The news is on before *I'm a Celebrity* starts and I let the doom and gloom wash over me in the same way as I let the taste of my tepid luxury seafood pie wash over my tastebuds helped down with a passable white. Then an image on the screen arrests my futile attempt to pretend I'm enjoying this meal. I make a grab for the remote and turn up the sound.

'*World famous Italian artist, Marcello Firenz, is in London this week for his first exhibition in five years . . .*'

I tune out as I see Marcello on my television screen, in my lounge. I'd know him anywhere. He speaks into the microphone that a reporter has thrust into his handsome face, but I don't hear what he's saying – I simply watch his hands rake through his dark curls and remember a time when my hands did the same thing. Marcello's face disappears and the newscaster moves onto another story. *Famous* Italian artist. I know Marcello Firenz's name – who doesn't? – but I had no inkling that he was *my* Marcello.

My heart's pounding as I jump up and search for this week's issue of *London Lifestyle*. Flicking wildly through the pages, I come to the events section. My eyes scan the listings until I see Marcello's name. And, sure enough, there it is. His exhibition opens to the public tomorrow night at a gallery that I've never heard of. My pounding heart halts abruptly. The exhibition is called Carnival.

I have no idea how I get through the next day at the office. I can't wait to get to Marcello's exhibition. My smartest suit has been hauled out of the back of my wardrobe and I've retouched my make-up a thousand times. I've spent so much time in the ladies' loos that my colleagues probably think I've got some hideous stomach bug. The ruby-red carnival masque is in a Sainsbury's carrier bag, plumes spilling over the top. I've taken it out and looked at it as many times as I've put more slap on. The afternoon drags interminably and the minute the hands of my watch hit six o'clock, I'm outta there. I take the packed, rush-hour Tube to the chi-chi gallery which is in a smart backstreet in Bloomsbury. There's a gaggle of people, champagne in hand, clustered round the door. I pull up short as I approach. In the window is a magnificent, full-size painting of a harlequin in a carnival masque, bright, vibrant, dancing. Despite the cold, my palms are clammy with sweat.

Pushing through the crowd, I make my way into the spacious white rooms. A waiter thrusts a glass of champagne into my hand and I down it gratefully. Juggling my carrier bag with its escaping plumes, I take some tiny canapés from a tray and eat them without tasting. Marcello must be here, surely, but I can't see him anywhere. He never did call me and, to be truthful, I never really expected him to.

The first room is filled with large canvasses of revellers in gaudy costumes; men in luscious capes wearing masques with obscenely pointed noses; women, breasts spilling from their lace-adorned dresses, cover their eyes with feline masques. My mouth is dry as I marvel at Marcello's skill. Murmurs of approval ripple through the crowd around me. As I make my way through the rest of the gallery, the paintings get more erotic, the masques more elaborate, more sinister, more beguiling.

There's a crush to get into the final room. A buzz of appreciative murmurs hangs in the air. I slowly wind my way through the crowd, gradually picking my way forward.

'Excuse me, excuse me. Thank you. Excuse me.' Then when I finally manage to squeeze through the doorway and into the room, I get my first glimpse of what the art lovers are staring at. I freeze and stare myself.

That's me. Up there on the wall. Thirty feet wide and twenty feet high. My breathing stops, arrested in my chest. I go hot, cold, hot again. It's really me. I am magnificent, voluptuous, provocative, sex personified. My breasts are full and inviting. My thighs, milk white, parted. The red velvet is draped between my legs, veiling and yet accentuating the delights that lie below.

No wonder Marcello wanted me. I'm a whore, a jezebel, a harlot, a scarlet woman, a temptress offering her goods for her chosen man to try. Beneath the disguise of my carnival masque there's a hint of sensual, knowing smile. I never realised that I was such a fabulous being. Who'd have known that this darkly sexual person was locked inside of me!

Suddenly the crowd thins. I feel a hand at my elbow and spin round.

'She's a beauty, isn't she?'

My eyes widen and the room rocks slightly under my feet. This was the very last person I was expecting to see. 'Jerrard?' I manage to say. 'What are you doing here?'

'Admiring the artwork,' he replies coolly.

A gulp travels down my throat. I haven't seen Jerrard since he walked out on me, the week before I went to Venice. Not one single phone call to find out how I was faring. Not one single phone call to see if I had gone away without him. Well, now he knows that I did. Now he can tell that I had a rather interesting trip.

His eyes are locked on the painting. He's finding it hard to tear his attention back to the real-life me. My cheeks are hot and flushed. Good grief. What on earth is he going to say now? I hide my carrier bag behind my back. What would my former lover think if he knew, if he found out that I have that very masque with me?

'This guy is a genius, isn't he?'

I nod, mutely.

Jerrard sighs contentedly and there's wonder in his voice when he says, 'Every brush stroke on the canvas is vibrant, alive.'

'Mmm,' I agree vaguely. *Not quite as alive as the same woman standing next to you.* I just wish he'd make his comments now and we can get this over with. I've never much cared for Jerrard's

43

cat and mouse games. He must realise that this is what I did in Venice without him.

'What a beauty,' he breathes again.

And I am. I'm naked for all to see. Yet still some don't notice me. Jerrard and I were together for five years. I stare at him open-mouthed. Surely he must recognise those breasts, those thighs, that come-hither look from my eyes? Can he not see the woman he knew so intimately right in front of him?

Finally, Jerrard drags his eyes away from the painting and glances at me. 'I'm sorry I haven't called,' he says. 'I meant to.'

I shrug. It's patently obvious that he has absolutely no idea that this wanton woman displayed in front of him is me.

'I heard that you had a good time in Venice.'

'Yes. I did.' I let my gaze fall on the painting and smile.

'Did you like the art?'

'Fabulous. I learned a lot.'

'Did it rain?'

'On one particular day, it never stopped.'

'How terrible.'

'Not at all,' I say. 'I still managed to amuse myself.'

'Look, I'm sorry about what happened between us,' Jerrard says. 'Perhaps I was a little hasty.'

Ah. So, it hasn't worked out with the nubile young bit-of-stuff.

He takes my hand. 'Do you have plans? Can I take you to dinner?'

I glance up at the massive canvas again and I see a woman who's powerful, self-assured, independent, confident. This is a woman who could do anything. She could give up her dreary job, move from her dreary flat, find herself a wonderful man, have herself a wonderful life. This is a woman who could rule the world. I slip my fingers out of Jerrard's grasp. 'No,' I hear myself say, 'I don't think so.'

Jerrard looks put out.

'I loved you, Jerrard, but our time has passed. I'm a different woman now. And I don't believe that you ever really knew me.' How can I begin to explain to him that a man who knew me for barely an afternoon saw so much more in me than Jerrard ever would? One day I'll find a man who will see me like that once again.

At the front of the gallery, someone claps their hands. 'Ladies and gentlemen,' he says. 'Mr Marcello Firenz!'

Marcello takes centre stage. He's as strikingly handsome as I remember. 'Thank you for coming this evening,' he says. 'It is very good to be back in London after such a long time . . .'

As Marcello continues with his well-rehearsed speech, I turn and see that Jerrard has slipped away from me and I have no desire to go after him.

'So, be my guests,' Marcello continues. 'Have some champagne. Eat. Look at the paintings . . .'

The assembled audience applauds and then moves out into the other rooms of the gallery. Marcello has a clutch of people around him. It's now or never. Shall I go up to him and say hello, tell him that painting my portrait is the most wonderful thing that anyone has ever done for me, or should I just melt into the background? He's laughing, enjoying the plaudits, comfortable with the adoration of his admirers.

'I'd love to buy this painting,' I hear a man say to Marcello as the would-be collector gawps up at me on the wall. 'It's magnificent. Your best work.'

'Ah, this one,' Marcello says, his full mouth parting in a languid smile. 'This one is not for sale.'

The man moves away looking slightly disgruntled at having his retail therapy thwarted. Marcello is momentarily alone and I ought to take my chance. I inch forward – not the brazen harlot now, but shy and unsure. As I near him, a woman joins

Marcello at his side. She's dark-haired, beautiful and I wonder if he's painted her too. Perhaps she's his wife, maybe a lover. He slips his arm casually round her shoulders and plants a tender kiss on her forehead. I get a vision of his lips against mine and can almost taste his kiss. Ah, well. I should go.

Then, as I turn to leave, Marcello's eye catches mine. Electricity crackles between us. I smile, mouth 'thank you' at him and quickly make my way out of the gallery.

The night has turned cold as I step into the street, but it can't take away the warm glow I feel inside. I think of Marcello and of the glorious afternoon we spent together in Venice. It will always be one of my most precious memories. I'm still clutching my carrier bag with the masque inside. This beautiful disguise will serve as a treasured and tangible reminder. A tear comes to my eye, but I won't be unhappy. I wonder where the painting will hang, who will look at it and what they will think of the woman in the ruby-red carnival masque? I'll look back at the masque in my old age and think of a time when I was young, reckless, daring and extraordinarily beautiful, a time when a weekend in Venice changed my life.

Shorter Stories

When I first started out as a writer, lots of magazines and newspapers used to print short stories, but not so much now despite the fact that they're really popular with readers. The following four shorty-short stories were all written as five-minute coffee break tales for print. Sometimes the tight word constraint is a bit of a challenge as it's harder to write a shorter story than it is a longer one. They are the Instagram of the story world! So grab a coffee and a chocolate Hobnob and indulge yourself.

Hotel du Lac

I fled to Montreux to escape the indifference of a lover, taking refuge in the Eden Palace au Lac hotel which stands proudly on the edge of Lake Geneva. If it was good enough for famous novelist Anita Brookner, who based her most-loved book in the same hotel, then I assumed it would do the job for me.

The spring air by the lake was also sharp enough to clear a fuddled brain and do unspeakable things to city smoke-filled lungs. It was a good place to think. I sat on the terrace in the sunshine, wrapped up against the chill, drinking French coffee as dark and rich as molasses and wondered why it was impossible to get another person's heart to answer the rhythm of one's own. Whenever I saw him, mine did a salsa routine. His steadfastly refused to be budged above a funeral march. The relationship was young, but it hadn't stop me from falling too deeply, too soon.

I booked a moonlight cruise. A ridiculously romantic notion, destined to plunge me further into depression. I was the only woman dining alone among a cosy huddle of couples, holding hands across the table as the majestic boat swanned interminably around Lac Léman, as the French call it. My dinner was superb and every mouthful nearly choked me.

Wandering out onto the deck, I looked out across the tar-black water to the winking lights of Évian-les-Bains nestled on the edge of the south shore of the lake. It was a bad place to be alone.

'You look cold, *Mademoiselle*.'

I turned in time to see a man removing his jacket. Unwise in the frosty atmosphere. He paused before slipping it on my shoulders. I paused before accepting the gesture. His jacket was warm from his body and smelled of Hugo Boss cologne.

'Thank you.'

'Like me, you dine alone.'

'Yes.' I pulled the jacket round my shoulders to ward off the chill.

He raised an eyebrow. 'You do not have a lover?'

I was taken aback by his directness and didn't know how to answer. Did I have a lover or not? It was something I asked myself often in recent months.

'Join me for coffee.' Without waiting for my reply, he led me back inside. We sat at his table and talked.

His name was Yves. He was older than me. Ten years. More. He was French, from Paris, and ran his own company. Something to do with the media which sounded interesting. He, too, was staying at the Eden au Lac. At midnight, we said goodbye on the hotel stairs and I lay in my bedroom, watching the moon, wishing for the phone to ring. A call from England, not from another room.

Next morning, after breakfast, Yves was sitting out on the terrace. 'Join me.'

He gave me a tiny box of hand-made chocolates. 'In Switzerland you must eat chocolate.'

He ordered us both double espressos and we shared the chocolates as we watched the joyous colours of the early flowers nod their heads against the grey-white snow of Mont Blanc.

'Do you ski?' he asked.

'After a fashion,' I said.

'Come to Zermatt.'

I laughed at the idea. 'I can't. I haven't got anything with me.'

He shrugged. 'I will buy you all that you need.'

'No. No thanks.'

Another shrug. 'Why not?'

'I don't know you.'

'Then how do you know that you will not enjoy it?'

Later, we walked round the lake, dodging the dog-walkers and the in-line skaters and hired a motor boat from a man who might have given the lover I'd left behind lessons in indifference.

The boat broke down half way across the lake. We were marooned, floating aimlessly in the middle of the water, buffeted by the fickle wind-whipped tide. Too far out to call for help, too far to swim for the shore. The boat owner came to rescue us, eventually. At first we laughed, but then sat in silence as we were tugged along behind him back to the shore.

That night Yves and I had dinner at a small Italian restaurant. It was the time of the Asparagus Festival and we duly obliged by ordering a seasonal dish from the grinning patron who assumed we were lovers. Yves gave me a red rose that he bought from a seller with hair like a gypsy who came to the table and I wished that my heart didn't beat to a different drum.

Yves's hand curled around mine as we reached the hotel. 'I would like very much to kiss you.'

He tasted my lips before I pulled away and retreated to the resounding silence of my room.

The next morning there was a gift-wrapped box on our table on the terrace. 'Open it,' he said as I sat down.

Inside a sliver of exquisite gold waited patiently. I looked up at him. 'I can't take this.'

'I want you to have it.'

'I can't. I don't want to mislead you.'

He had a beautiful smile. 'Maybe I would like to be misled.'

'Really. It's too much.'

'Take it.' Yves wound the bracelet round my wrist and fastened it. 'Take it as a token from a man who, in different circumstances, you might have loved.'

'Yves . . .'

'I leave tomorrow.' He stood up. 'Don't wait for ever for a man who is a fool.'

I sat for a long time, twisting the slender gold strands on my wrist. I didn't want it to end like this. Perhaps I should go to Zermatt. After all, what was there to go home for? I would go back to my room and call Yves.

As I opened the door, the salsa rhythm in my heart kicked in once more. On the floor was a note from reception on crisp Eden au Lac headed paper. Neat. Precise. Efficient. It gave the time of the call. The name. The message.

I miss you, it said.

The Small Blue Box

We've had a difficult year, Alex and I. The downturn in the global economy, the credit crunch, the woman whose name he dropped into the conversation too often, have all adversely affected our relationship.

At one point, I didn't think that we were going to survive. My husband of five years was under threat of losing his job, the mortgage payments were soaring, our plastic was maxed, everything was piling up on top of us. No different, then, from a million other couples who had over-extended themselves on the crest of the feel-good wave. Nothing was too good for us, nothing beyond our budget. Now the bill had finally landed on the mat.

Then Alex's company was taken over by another in an aggressive buy-out. The worries on the job front escalated as hundreds were ruthlessly axed. Would we keep the roof over our heads? Would the Merc have to go?

Our fears for our future were, it seems, unfounded. Alex survived the swingeing rounds of cuts. He got on brilliantly with his new boss. Lauren. She thought he was wonderful. He told me often. Ten times a night she texted him. Work-related issues. Urgent ones. Though any subsequent phonecalls were taken in the study with the door firmly closed and my husband speaking in hushed tones.

Alex talked about her constantly – how great she was to

work for. I'm sure he looked forward too much to the weekends they had to work away in Rome, Amsterdam, Venice. I stayed at home and chewed anxiously at my fingernails.

The crunch came a month ago. After one too many late nights at the office, I accused Alex of having an affair with her. He laughed away my fears, told me I should be grateful that he'd still got a job that he loved, working with someone that he admired and respected as his superior. Besides, Lauren – he assured me – was portly, matronly, not the ambitious man-hungry sex-kitten I imagined. I laughed at my own fears.

Alex was more attentive immediately. He's even taken me away with him on this business trip. Something we used to do years ago, when love was young. You can't believe the relief in my heart. He didn't want to be away from me on my birthday, he said. So New York it is!

My husband is in back-to-back meetings, so I have the day to myself. In the morning I wrap up and take a long walk, stopping to listen to a writer talking about her book in the open air library in Bryant Park while sipping a takeaway cappuccino. Ms Zelda Bayliss is one of those single, high-maintenance and interminably shrill women that New York do so well. Multiply unlucky in love, borderline unhinged, she's now writing self-help manuals for desperate divorcees with a degree of commercial success. As I listen to her, I think of how fortunate I am to have Alex. We've had our bumpy times, but our love is stronger for it.

After lunch at the Carnegie Deli, I swing down Fifth Avenue feeling alive, rejuvenated in the cold, fresh air. All the windows are impeccably dressed for the coming spring and my heart swells with joy. A new start, I think with a smile. I'm loved and I'm in love. Then, ahead of me, at the crosswalk, I see a familiar figure. In all of New York, my husband is less than a hundred metres in front of me.

Alex has his collar up against the cold, but I'd recognise him anywhere. I call him, but my voice is lost in the noise of the street, the honking of horns, the high-octane thrum of traffic and people. Then I hold my breath when I see where he's headed. My husband disappears through the doors of Tiffany's and it's all that I can do not to chase after him.

My knees go weak. After all that we've been through he must be keen to spoil me and this is more than I could ever have dreamed of. Alex knows that I'd love a piece of Tiffany jewellery for my birthday. This would truly be symbolic that our troubles were over and I can't believe that he's being so thoughtful.

I huddle in a shop doorway, hiding until I see him come out. There's a smile on his lips and one of those famous blue boxes in his hand. He pockets it then jauntily crosses the street again. I want to run after him, throw myself in his arms, but I don't want to spoil his surprise with one of my own.

The hotel is perfect. Our suite sumptuous. Alex has dinner sent to the room. He doesn't want the hustle and bustle of busy restaurant. He wants me all to himself, he says.

The exquisite food is served by the vast window with a panoramic view over the city below. We glow romantically together in the flickering candlelight. I keep a lid on my impatience, waiting excitedly for my expensive Tiffany present. Surely he'll give it to me now? I can hardly bear the suspense. Dessert is a glorious chocolate mousse. We spoon it into each other's mouths, giggling like lovestruck teenagers. And, after I've eaten every morsel, Alex pulls out a gift-wrapped box with a theatrical flourish.

He takes my hands and kisses them tenderly. 'Happy birthday, darling,' he says.

The tiny pink hearts blur in front of me as I thank him profusely for the red lace underwear he's bought for me. My heart bangs loudly in my chest. Who is the lucky recipient of the Tiffany bag, I wonder? Lauren, my husband's boss, who he has so stoutly denied? Or is there someone else deserving of expensive jewellery?

Later, we make love twenty-seven floors above Manhattan. Me in the tacky undies, my husband more naked to me than I ever wanted to see him.

Alex pours chilled champagne for me as I lie in his arms and we laugh. I laugh the loudest, but it can't mask my sadness. I sound shrill, borderline unhinged, like the writer in Bryant Park. As I struggle to keep the tears at bay, to pretend that everything is just as it was, I realise that I love my husband more than ever. Even though the small blue Tiffany box never appears and my knees feel weak once more.

Love in a Slightly Chilly Climate

'Ooo. It's certainly very big, Alistair.' My eyes widen involuntarily.

'I think you'll enjoy this, Clara.' Alistair settles himself and smiles.

I want to get this straight before we start. It's not one of *those* sorts of stories. There's nothing torrid here. None of that squelchy stuff. Certainly not. I'm talking about the movie screen, that's what's big. Nothing else. It's looming large, in front of us, filling my vision. Four storeys high with forty Dolby speakers to deliver state-of-the-art sound. Whatever that means. That it's ear-splittingly loud, it seems. *IMAX – Not just a film, a movie experience!* Well, I'll be the judge of that.

This is a rare outing. We don't come to London very often. Alistair and I don't like the noise or the fumes or the litter. And the trains never run on time. You have to leave hours and hours spare, just in case. Great Linley, our little village, offers us a peaceful, sheltered existence and it suits us. It suits us perfectly. We wouldn't have lived there for so many years if it hadn't, would we?

But this is a treat for Alistair. It's the fiftieth anniversary of the successful summitting of Mount Everest and we've come along today to watch tiny, ant-like men in lurid anoraks trudge up slopes that are too steep for words. They're snaking in a long, unwieldy queue just to get up the mountain – it's worse than late-nite shopping in Sainsbury's. I hate that – 'nite'. Why can't they use 'night' like everyone else? Everything has to be new-fangled and mucked about with now.

Alistair likes to read about men overcoming great challenges. Sea, land or air. It doesn't matter. He has dozens of books on Everest. Dozens and dozens. He doesn't want to go there, of course. That would be silly. We're not that kind of people. But it doesn't stop us admiring courage in others.

Though this does seem like a monumental struggle, I have to say. Every step looks like pure torture to me. They have to use bottled oxygen as their bodies start to die the nearer they get to the top – so the narrator informs us. I can never under-stand why people would risk their lives for a moment of glory on top of a mountain – albeit the highest mountain in the world. Why on earth do you need to do that when you can sit in a comfortable cinema and watch a perfectly nice film about it? Life's hard enough without putting yourself through that sort of thing. I'm not a stranger to struggle though. Oh no. Not on the scale of these adventurers in UV goggles and Polartec trousers, obviously. Small struggles in the scheme of things. But struggles, nevertheless.

We have Alistair's mother living with us – which is never an easy situation, is it? Don't get me wrong, she's a lovely woman. Lovely. It's just that she's ever so slightly . . . well . . . I daren't say it out loud . . . *mad*. We have to be very careful with her. She keeps her dentures in a glass of vodka, which she drinks during the night. But she has no idea that we know and, quite honestly, we prefer to keep it that way. Recently, we caught her *tiddling* on the cabbages in our beloved vegetable patch. Which is not a problem in itself. Thankfully, the neighbours can't see her as we have a secluded garden. Very nice, south-facing. But I couldn't be sure she hadn't *relieved* herself on any other produce. I couldn't bring myself to touch a carrot. Just in case.

A whole season's crop went to waste. And Alistair and I don't like to waste food. You don't when there are starving people everywhere, do you? I've never planted anything since. It has quite spoiled the joy of horticulture.

And Alistair has never had the promotion he deserves. Another minor struggle. It doesn't affect him '24/7' – as they say now. But from nine o'clock to five o'clock it can be quite a problem. He simply won't get involved in office politics. No one understands that these days. He's not considered a 'team player' because he doesn't like to spend his weekend paintballing or go-karting and all the other 'bonding' activities the management like to organise. What man over the age of fifty-five does? The garden would go to pot while he was out there shooting Rodney Jones from accounts. Although that wouldn't be a bad thing, if it were a real gun. That man is the bane of Alistair's life. He's the bean-counter *extraordinaire*. He sees having ethics as a weakness, not a virtue. Alistair is wasted at that company. I tell him all the time.

Not that Alistair's perfect. Oh, I used to think he was. A long time ago. When we were first married, I used to hang on his every word. Now I'm more likely to notice the food that hangs on the corner of his mouth when he's eating or that he slurps when he drinks his tea and that he shouts at the Spanish waiters when we're on holiday. He can be very embarrassing. Without trying, really. But I should be grateful. Everyone else my age seems to be single. I work at the local doctor's surgery. As a receptionist. It's a very important role. Everyone needs doctor's receptionists. My colleagues are all single. Born-again singletons, they laugh. They've all been left by their husbands, of course. Invariably for younger models. Even Helena Browne and, quite frankly, her husband's nothing to write home about. They all pick over their married years like vultures. But they do it too loudly and for too long and I think it's not as easy living alone as they make out. I try not to mention how much Alistair does for me. They must all have to go and put petrol in their own cars now. That must be simply awful.

Up on the screen, the men are crossing a yawning crevasse. I can hardly bear to look. It's overwhelming. Speaking of yawning, I check to see if Alistair's still awake, even though I can't hear any tell-tale snoring. Once he persuaded me to go to the cinema recently to watch a 'boys' film. Some awful thing with cowboys running round. After half an hour Alistair was fast asleep. I left and got a taxi home. The first thing my husband knew about it was some hair-gelled youth waking him up when it was all over, so that he could clear the seats and tidy away the discarded popcorn cartons. Not *our* popcorn cartons – we don't like to snack in public. Anyway, Alistair was mortified. I've never let him forget it. Surreptitiously, I glance towards him. His eyes are going heavy now. Even with all this excitement going on. I give him a nudge. He grunts and refocuses on the screen while I study my husband of thirty-something years.

He's still a handsome man, for all his advancing years. Not too much grey, not too much paunch. Not really. We still have passion in our lives. Not a lot of it. But we make love on Sunday mornings – not *every* Sunday, obviously – to the rhythmic sound of Alan, the man next door, mowing the lawn. I think Alan would be rather shocked if he knew what we were up to. Or maybe he'd take a little more time with his strimming or move closer to our boundary hedge. We're not ravers, though. I don't want to give that impression. If there's a swinging set in Great Linley, I'm afraid Alistair and I aren't part of it. The Bridge Club is saucy enough for us. I've never in my life entertained the idea of pink, furry handcuffs being a prerequisite for sexual fun. That's not to say that I don't have my moments. I have come very close to being swept off my feet – not by Alistair, I must hasten to add. Only recently a man came into my surgery for an appointment and when I looked at him, the whole world stopped. It just ceased turning. The noise from the screaming children in the waiting room stilled and there was just me and him and a rushing of blood in my ears. He'd come for an injection – a series of them – he was going somewhere exotic. I can't remember where. Maybe he was going to climb a mountain. He looked the type. Rugged, strong, resilient. Not troubled by the normal cares of the world. And I wondered, just for a fleeting moment what it would be like to have those strong arms around me, to be taken by him – and I mean *taken* – possibly even *outside* in our secluded, south-facing garden. Before my mother-in-law spoiled it by using it as a public convenience. And he knew. He knew that he'd turned my legs to a consistency not conducive to standing up. He gave me a slow burning smile that, well, I'm ashamed to admit this, *undressed* me! It was then when I had my first menopausal hot flush. I could have done with my own supply of bottled oxygen, I'll tell you. Still, it was a passing thing. He hasn't been in since. I did wonder if he'd start to make up mystery illnesses just to pop in and see me, make appointments he wouldn't keep in order to hear my voice. But he didn't. And I can't say that I'm sorry. It's not that I'm unhappy with Alistair – *au contraire* – he has served me very well for many a year. But it doesn't hurt to dream, does it? It doesn't hurt to think what might have been. Dreams only become a bit tricky when you start to expect them to become real life. It was a moment, a millisecond of recklessness. Where would we be if doctor's receptionists handed in their notices every day to follow dark-haired, dark-eyed strangers round the world on a whim?

Our heroes on the screen are edging closer to their goal, ice-picks in hand, inching along a knife-edge ridge high above the fluffy clouds, edging closer to their dream. There's something selfish and indulgent in climbing a mountain for the sheer hell of it, just because it's there. I do worry sometimes that our universe is becoming smaller while the whole world outside is becoming easier and easier to conquer. A man holds a flag up and they've made it. As we all knew they would. Cheers all round. Some of the audience burst into spontaneous applause. How American. Perhaps they are Americans. Surely they can't be British.

We get up and shuffle to the exit, taking our rubbish with us. If only more people would do that, the world would be a nicer place.

Alistair looks slightly dazed. 'That was rather good.'

It was.

'Jolly heroic.' My husband's face holds an envious look. 'Wish I'd done something like that in my youth.' Try as I might I cannot see Alistair in a day-glo yellow anorak and goggles. Besides, he doesn't like heights. Alistair could get vertigo on the top of a double-decker bus – something else that has been consigned to the dustbin in the name of progress. Perhaps if we'd been blessed with children, it could have been one of our sons up there braced against the elements five miles above the earth. But well . . . it never happened. Another of life's little struggles that we coped with together. And we have Benny, a wee Westie, who brings us a lot of pleasure.

'I wish I was more . . .' Alistair purses his lips. 'You know . . .'

'I like you just the way you are.' And he likes me just the way I am – despite me not being one of Slimming World's roaring successes. We're comfortable with each other. Something very underrated in this day and age. If you're not swinging from the chandeliers every night or share the same taste in Fromage Frais you can't have a good marriage according to the *Daily Mail*. Well, what we have suits us.

'I'm freezing cold just looking at all that snow.' Alistair shivers

61

and rubs his arms, making a joke of it. I laugh. He can be a very funny man. Not always intentionally. 'Let's go and find a nice café and have a lovely cup of tea.'

He takes my arm and links it through his, giving it a small squeeze. I give him a peck on the cheek, even though we're now out on the street and there are other people around.

'That'll warm us up,' I agree. And, do you know, it always does.

Coffee at the Café de Paris

I go back to the Café de Paris. Sometimes. Not often. But if you saw it you'd wonder why I ever went there at all. Really, you would.

They serve passable pastries. Sometimes they're fresh and crisp. Sometimes they are just crisp, giving a hint of two-day-old staleness which detracts somewhat from the sheer joy of the excess of calories. They dole out a mediocre cappuccino that tastes slightly too bitter and the brilliant white froth carries the synthetic look of shaving foam and disappears too rapidly revealing the insipid brownness that lurks beneath. If I were being clever I'd say that it reminded me of something else. Something else that faded far too fast. Something else white and wonderful that eventually turned beige. But I'm not feeling clever today, just a little sad.

The Café de Paris is always crowded, despite its reputation for hygienic indifference and a charming reluctance to serve customers – possibly the only connection with its glamorous namesake. It's amazing how these places survive, isn't it? But they do. I sit down under the rainbow-coloured awning which has streaky lines faded by sun and patches of mildew as if it can't quite decide which one it wants to expire from first.

It's raining today, as it was when I first came here, and the drips run down the candy stripes, scamper across the rain-soaked pavement and join the gurgling stream which has swelled in the gutter. I shake the drips from my umbrella and toss it on the floor at my feet, careless that it will get even wetter. When the vaguely disinterested waitress eventually arrives, I order a coffee but can't bring myself to risk the eclectic nature of their fayre. And, besides, my stomach isn't quite right today. It has that hungry, searching feeling which is nothing to do with lack of food. I know what its desires are, as much as I know that they are out there somewhere beyond its reach.

I probably don't even need to tell you that this involves a man. Doesn't it always? I probably don't even need to tell you that for weeks, months, years, I couldn't come near this place at all. The coffee was always as bitter, impatient customers still jostled with equally impatient waitresses to get to the tables, the music was just the same, melancholy laments that reminded me too well of the one thing that was missing.

But you don't know about that yet, so let me fill you in. Okay. Here goes. This is where I met Sebastian. This ill-tempered, unsatisfactory little haven was where I first met my love. The man that was about to blow my world apart and fill my dreams. Don't the most awful places seem to be the ones that hold the best, the dearest memories?

It was pouring down, we were both running, I guess, to escape the rain and we careered into the one remaining pavement table at the exact same moment. Is that fate or what?

We both laughed and I shook my umbrella in a much more flirty way than I did earlier. Sebastian said we should sit together and I saw no reason not to. I was young, free and single – or alternatively read bored, lonely and broke – and the light in Sebastian's cornflower-blue eyes brightened up the dull, cloudy day with a sky that loomed above us painted battleship grey.

He had dark wavy hair which curled damply over his forehead and he ran his fingers through it trying to smooth it down which made it even more wayward and I thought how much I would like to do it for him. I couldn't believe the things we talked about. I know this is so corny and how many times you must have heard it before? You're going to tut when you read it, I know you are. But you've been there too. Don't deny it.

I felt like I had known him all my life. His startling eyes saw inside me, like no one else's had ever done before. He listened to me. I know its not much to ask, but how often does someone really listen to you? And he laughed at my jokes. Which, if you'd ever heard me tell a joke, you'd appreciate is a really big deal. He was so open and honest and he had a gentle warm laugh that pattered like the rain on the canvas above us. We were the only people giggling as everyone else huddled miserably in the cold, eking out their lukewarm drinks until the rain stopped.

By the end of our third cup, his hand had somehow inched across the table and his fingertips covered mine. When the rain eventually ceased and the merest sliver of sun split the clouds we left. Together. Sebastian grabbed my hand and we walked the wet street pretending to window-shop when neither of us saw anything else but each other. Occasionally we would point out insignificant trinkets to give us the excuse to stop and surreptitiously touch.

We made love that night in his bed and his hair curled damply on his forehead again as he gasped my name in ecstatic breaths. When we woke, wound together, the next morning, I learned that he hated his dark, dishevelled curls. But I loved them. I always did. It reminded me of when we made love and when we first met. Whenever I think of him, I think of him like that.

I am getting chilly deep down inside sitting here and I want another drink, but in true Café de Paris style, I cannot attract anyone's attention. This also where, five years later, Sebastian told me he had met someone else. Has anyone ever said that to you? It turns your blood to ice instantly, believe me.

A waitresses jogs me as she passes by with coffee for another couple who are sitting sheltering from the rain. They are in love and they don't care who knows it. I remember it well and now I am sitting here drinking cold coffee for one, wondering how you can be like that then suddenly without warning it's gone. I never knew what was wrong and never got a chance to put it right. That's what hurts the most.

We had rowed. I don't know what about. What do you bicker about in relationships that have lasted for five years? Things that were so important that you now can't recall them at all. We went for a walk to calm down and I suggested we came here. I should have known better, but I had no idea I was under threat of extinction. So, we were squabbling. Couples do, don't they? Sometimes.

We drank the only decent cup of coffee we'd ever had here in sullen silence and then he told me that he loved me, but he couldn't go on. Just like that. He loved her too much to give her up. He was torn. *He was torn!* He who had just ripped my heart into little shreds was torn.

He drained his cold, cold coffee and left. Left me there alone with my crumby plate and my half-eaten chocolate fancy and my half-drunk coffee on a hot, sunny day that held no warmth. I watched him go gladly, spite in my heart, wishing him ill, and I felt like that for ages. Two weeks, at least. For two weeks my vitriol kept me from feeling. And then, after that, I missed him with a pain that I never previously knew existed.

All trace of him had gone from my flat, taken to another life. Another life without me. I had screwdrivers stuck under my ribs and a spin dryer battering the insides of my stomach and the noise of chalk screeching down a blackboard permanently inside my head. Everyone describes it differently, but it's just the same for all of us, isn't it? All of us who have loved so desperately and deeply and have lost.

I heard later that she had left him. I love these cruel little tricks fate has a habit of playing, don't you? Now Sebastian knew just what it felt like to be alone. But it didn't bring him back to me.

Life goes on, doesn't it? It has to. I stopped listening to soppy music. I couldn't watch anything with Tom Hanks in it. I carried a permanent supply of damp Kleenex. I couldn't come to the Café de Paris. You know how it is.

Since then, I have had three other men in my life. An Edward, a Dairmud and a Cameron. An Englishman, an Irishman and a Scotsman. There must be a joke in there somewhere, but I can't find it today. And, anyway, its not that bad considering that there are very few decent single men out there. I had a lot of fun. Once, I even thought I might have been in love. But no one touched my heart, my life, like Sebastian. It was as if there was a piece of my jigsaw missing and not just one of the bits at the edge that doesn't spoil the picture. The bit that was missing was slap-bang in the middle. It still is. Everyone could see my loss. And try as I might to disguise it, you really couldn't miss it.

But here I am again today. Even though the Café de Paris may not have changed, I believe I have. I listen to love songs once more. Some days I even sing along. I know that I have loved to my limit and have been loved in return. And Sebastian really did love me. Once upon a time, a long time ago.

I smile to myself. I think I will give up on my quest for fresh coffee. The rain looks like it is easing off anyway and I have things that I must do. Not exciting things, but things nevertheless. I have a list in my pocket to remind me. I don't remember everything as well as I do Sebastian.

I look down to the floor, trying to locate my sodden umbrella and when I look up again, he is standing there. His collar is up because of the rain and his hair is a curled, gorgeous mess.

His cheeks are pink with the exertion of running or, perhaps, embarrassment and we both look at each other open-mouthed and breathless for different reasons.

'Anna,' he says.

'I was just leaving.'

'Don't.' His eyes plead with me and he sits down at my table running his fingers through his hair.

'I didn't know you still came here.'

'I do sometimes. When I need to think.' He looks round taking in the drabness and the surly staff. His lips twitch with humour. 'It's still awful, isn't it?'

'Yes.' I laugh and it sounds strong and clear.

Sebastian laughs too and I realise I could still lose myself in those eyes. And I think, perhaps, I'd better go now before I do.

He lowers his dark, damp lashes. 'You look great,' he says and glances at my empty cup. 'It's been a long time.'

It hardly seems like yesterday to me, but I say nothing.

'Stay for another cup.'

'If we can get served.' I try to sound cool and unconcerned, but my traitorous fingers let my umbrella fall to the floor.

His hand edges uncertainly across the table, his fingers find mine and entwine with them. He crushes them slightly and I never want it to stop. 'This is just like old times,' he says and there is a hopeful note in his voice.

He smiles and do you know what? The rain stops. The rain stops falling in the street and in my heart.

'Yes,' I say. And, despite the best efforts of the Café de Paris, I know the next cup of coffee will taste close enough to perfect for me.

About Gardening

I am planting primulas. Not my favourite flower. Their colours are hard and garish, false, man-made and their stubby little leaves are too bright and chunky. I am planting them in regimental rows like soldiers in their dress uniforms, because I need form and structure in my life, rows and rituals to get me through my days.

This is not a *Ground Force* garden where things are planted in drifts or appealing groups of three for maximum impact. There is no natty watercolour painting lurking in the background to show me how it's supposed to look. This garden is a mess, built haphazardly over the years with no thought to where it all might be leading and with a lack of regular tender, loving care that leaves it teetering on the brink of neglect. This garden is the 'before' of a 'before and after' feature.

I leave a gap between each one so that they stand quite alone, self-sufficient, unable to touch the next plant even if they really wanted to. My husband, Sam, bought the plants at our local garden centre, because they were going cheap and because, presumably, he thought we needed something in lurid pink to brighten our lives. We are trying to be nice to each other and after ten years of marriage that's sometimes very hard.

We were too young when we married. We considered having an Elvis look-alike marry us in Las Vegas and I think that says a lot about how seriously we viewed our vows. Instead, I wore a black mini-dress and we left the register office in Clapham, squashed into a friend's ancient Morris Minor with balloons streaming from the back and beaming smiles, but even then I knew it would be a struggle. Our relationship had been on and off more times than a bulimic's fridge light and we weren't happy enough with ourselves to be able to make anyone else happy. After ten years we don't even have a joint bank account as if we are both still coming to terms with the idea of permanency. We don't screw anything into the wall as if we are always worried that we might have to take it down. We own nothing jointly, apart from an ageing, ill-tempered car, and I don't know if this is how married couples should behave. You may wonder why I'm still here. I do. Frequently.

Sam is so handsome – when the strain of holding everything together isn't etched into his face – and it isn't easy to turn your back on shared lives. No matter how little they resemble Hollywood ideals. I know where I will be next Christmas. I have an address book stuffed with mutual friends. Sam and I share a PC and I haven't a clue how to find half of my files without him. These small domestic markers bind us together, so one year flows seamlessly into the next without me ever finding the words I think I want to say.

I practise them. When I am planting primulas, for example. I am leaving you, Sam. I need space. But then I think that makes me sound like Captain Kirk. And, anyway, I have a lot of space. Too much space. Sam plays golf and squash and bridge. I sing and do Tai Chi and am supposed to be the gardener. We do very little together. Except watch television. And there's never anything on these days, is there?

We make love still. A miracle perhaps when we hardly ever touch. But it leaves us lying on our backs looking at the ceiling and as far apart as these wretched primulas.

The light is fading and my fingers are becoming cold and

cramped in the soil. I really must do something about this garden before it swamps me and I can never hack my way out of it at all.

I can't just continue to sit here tinkering with the surface, planting pretty plants to make it look all right, when there is a jungle of weeds threatening to engulf me at any minute. Yet the thought of tearing it all down and rebuilding another bigger, better, improved garden leaves me breathless with pain. Perhaps that's why they always blub at the end of *Ground Force*. Perhaps it is the sheer relief that someone else has done all the hard work for them. The lovely Alan Titchmarsh comes along and takes away the fear that you might tear it all apart and get it completely and hopelessly wrong again next time.

I stand up and stretch my back. Looking down at the primulas from a distance, they don't look so bad and I promise that I'll water them regularly so that they at least have half a chance of survival. Nurturing is not my strong point. But at least I know it.

Plodding up the garden in the deepening gloom, I brush the soil from my hands and, after kicking off my wellies on the kitchen step, go inside. A waft of comforting steam laden with the tang of warm spices greets me. Sam has my apron on and is stirring something thoughtfully with a wooden spoon.

'It's your favourite.' He tastes whatever it is. 'I think.'

I press my lips together and ease the word I want to say from my throat. 'Thanks.'

'They look okay.' Sam glances out of the window at the garden. 'The pansies.'

'They're primulas.'

'Right,' he says and, like the flowers, his eyes are too bright. He turns away and stirs his pot again. 'I'll help you out there tomorrow. If you want. We can make a start on clearing it.'

'Yes,' I say. 'I'd like that.'

71

I cross to the cooker and brush my dirty, cold fingers across his lips. Sam closes his eyes as he kisses them and I leave a smut of soil on his mouth which he doesn't wipe away. I can feel my hot tears prickle behind my eyes as if I'm going to do the *Ground Force* weeping thing. And I know that it's because we can make the new, improved, bigger, better version if we want to. If we both want to.

It wouldn't be a complete collection of short stories for me if it didn't include one about chocolate. Since I wrote The Chocolate Lovers series of books – which are firm favourites with my readers – I've been a chocoholic. Plus I've always been a keen baker, but even more so since the advent of *The Great British Bake Off*. Those of you who follow me on Facebook and Twitter will be well aware of how much I love it.

My lovely nana worked in a bakehouse from the age of twelve and was a fabulous cook. There was always something wonderful and warm in the oven at her house – an apple pie or a crumble. In the school holidays, she used to try to teach me how to bake – though it was always 'just a pinch of this' and 'a handful of that'. She was one of the generation of bakers who didn't possess scales and I think she'd like it if she could see now that I'd taken over the baking mantle in the family. Though I'm definitely the sort of baker who has to follow a recipe.

If you've been a fan of my Chocolate Lovers books, then you'll be pleased to know that I'd love to write some more. I love those ladies and can't leave them alone. Plus it will be the perfect excuse to eat lots of lovely chocolate and call it research.

The Way to a Man's Heart

When James left me, I cut my hair and changed my career. Packing in my job was scary, but very liberating. For the last ten years, the accounts department at the local council offices has been my security blanket – a rather dull one, admittedly, but secure nevertheless. No one thought that reliable old Maddy Knight would have the courage to quit. Least of all me.

I bought an ancient burger van from eBay, spent the weekend painting it a gorgeous shade of deep chocolate brown, called myself Chocoholics Anonymous and got a pitch at three different local markets. I've wanted to do it for years, but we all get comfortable in our velvet-lined ruts, don't we? It takes some cataclysmic change in our circumstances to give us the courage to make that necessary move.

In my newly painted eBay ex-burger van, I sell muffins, brownies, chocolate chip cookies – whatever takes my fancy, whatever chocolate delights I think will lure customers to my window. I don't expect that I'm going to earn enough to be able to retire early to the Bahamas, but it's fair to say that business is booming.

As you can see, I'm trying to move on. I'm doing all the things that the broken-hearted are supposed to do in my situation. It is, however, rather difficult when James is still living in the flat above me and I'm still in love with him.

Since James left me, I spend my long, lonely evenings melting, blending, baking, preparing my wares for the next day. Opening my oven, I slide out a tray of chocolate muffins and the decadent scent of baking chocolate fills my kitchen. I close my eyes and inhale deeply. Heavenly aromas of vanilla and cocoa float on the air. The muffins, rich and moist, spill temptingly over their paper cases, making my mouth water.

As I'm taking my time selecting which muffin I should sample, my doorbell rings.

James is standing there.

'Hi,' he says.

His hair is ruffled, untidy and I long to smooth it down, feel its softness beneath my fingers once again. 'Hi.'

My ex-boyfriend is uncomfortable. We haven't spoken to each other in weeks and he certainly hasn't rung my doorbell since he told me that he wanted time to himself, to think about where he was going and what he wanted from life. The subtext being that what he wanted from life clearly wasn't me.

'I just thought I'd drop by to see how you are,' James tells me.

'Fine,' I say with a carefree shrug. I'm not. I'm terrible. I love him. I miss him. I will him to understand this without me saying it. I want my pain to be conveyed through the ether to him.

'Cool.' He nods, thoughtfully.

Then a waft of the freshly baked cakes drifts out of the door, like a curl of smoke from a genie's bottle.

James sniffs the air. 'Wonderful,' he says. 'What's cooking?'

'Oh.' I wave a hand towards the kitchen. 'Chocolate muffins. For my new business venture.'

'I heard about that.'

From one of our mutual friends, I presume. Friends who are now having to consider which one of us they invite to dinner, to parties, to celebrations.

'You can come in and have one if you like.' I try not to sound too hopeful, but I know that James is a complete sucker for my baking. Always was. He can't have changed that much in a few weeks. I know the way to that man's heart. Or, at least, I thought I did.

A smile flits across his face. 'Wow. Chocolate muffins,' he says with a wistful sigh. 'My favourites.'

'Do you have time?'

He checks his watch, but it's an unconvincing gesture. 'Maybe I could just have one.'

I go back inside and James follows me into the kitchen where he lurks just inside the doorway.

'Take your coat off,' I instruct while I choose the fullest, tastiest-looking muffin and hand it to him. 'Do you want a coffee with it?'

'Mmm,' James murmurs as he bites into the muffin. 'Good grief, this is marvellous.'

'Thanks.' I put his coffee down on the table. 'Sit down. If you're not in a rush.'

He lowers his long, rangy frame into the chair. Maybe he's thinner now that he's living on takeaway dinners for one rather than my home-cooked meals.

'Another muffin?'

'Yes, please,' James says and I know that I have him in my thrall once more.

In my Chocoholics Anonymous van, I sell out of the chocolate muffins before the morning is over. A big hit. I must make more of them for next week. My white chocolate éclairs have all gone too, plus the heart-shaped chocolate biscotti. I can hardly keep pace with the demand for my chocolate banoffee pies. If business carries on like this, then I'm going to have to draft in someone to help me with the baking.

It's a bitterly cold day and sales of my hot chocolate with a hint of chilli and a generous topping of whipped cream are brisk. Builders are renovating an old house at the end of the street, turning it into exclusive offices. They're among my most dedicated customers, coming for an order two or three times a day. Today, they've completely cleaned me out of chewy chocolate and nut cookies. I'll have to increase my output. Though I've got a warm glow inside me, I rub my hands together to keep them warm.

The next night, James rings my doorbell once more. 'Boy, they smell good.'

His gaze is falling on the kitchen door.

'Marbled brownies,' I say as I lean casually on the door frame. 'Cream cheese swirled through a dark chocolate sponge. I've just this minute lifted them out of the oven.'

'Oh,' he breathes.

'Want some?'

James is unwinding his scarf before he's even come through the front door. My kitchen is already laden with cakes, cookies and biscuits ready for the next day.

James is on his second coffee and his third brownie when he says, 'There was something I meant to tell you yesterday.' He tentatively picks the last remaining chocolate crumbs from his plate. 'I'm seeing someone else.'

The fork that I'm holding clatters to the floor and I fumble with picking it up.

'I thought I'd better let you know,' James continues, looking slightly abashed. 'I wouldn't want you to bump into Claire on the stairs and it be, well, embarrassing for you.'

'No, no.' I shake my head. 'We wouldn't want that.'

James looks relieved. 'She's lovely,' he tells me as if I should be pleased for him. 'But I'll never find anyone who bakes like you do, Maddy.'

'Another brownie?' I say.

I see Claire on the stairs a few days later. I'm taking boxes of cappuccino cheesecake down to the cool boxes in the Chocoholics Anonymous van ready for tomorrow when she's making her way up to James's apartment. She smiles uncertainly at me, as well she might. Clearly James has told her about the ex-girlfriend who lives downstairs.

I wonder has he also told her that he's now popping into my place every night to taste my chocolate cakes. He's given up his regular evening run to make time to visit me, so I make sure that he isn't disappointed. On Tuesday it was chocolate cheesecake with salted caramel topping; Wednesday was honey and milk chocolate heart biscuits; Thursday was chocolate-coated flapjack. Tonight James had four slices of rocky road. He comes to me on his way home from work, stays for an hour, eats all the cakes I give him and then rushes off to be with her.

Claire is blonde, pretty, slender. My love's new girlfriend looks like she spends a lot of time in the gym and as if chocolate never passes her rosebud lips. She looks like she exists solely on lollo rosso, rocket and watercress.

'Hello,' she says, shyly.

'Hi,' I reply. 'I'm James's neighbour, Maddy.'

'He's told me a lot about you.'

I wonder if he's told her that she fails to live up to my standards in the baking department? I wonder what else I do better than her and what she does better than me.

Ladenham has an old-fashioned high street, spoiled only by the rash of charity shops, estate agents and banks. The market is thriving as it's home to an organic butcher and a man who comes with freshly baked bread and homemade pickles. There's an excellent cheese stall too. The elderly ladies who frequent the market love my spicy white hot chocolate flavoured with cardamom – a dusting of cocoa powder

78

sifted on the top. They crowd round my Chocoholics Anonymous van and chatter about their grandchildren and buy giant chocolate cookies with Smarties on the top to take away for them.

'We wish you were here every market day, Maddy,' they chorus as they leave.

Smiling to myself, I think I might look on eBay tonight – when James has eaten his fill of my cakes and gone to be with Claire – to see if I can find another dilapidated vehicle to do up. I'd need another assistant to man that van, but we could cover twice the pitches, visit twice as many markets, sell twice as many chocolate delights. I've got a rotund middle-aged lady called Martha who now comes in to help me bake three days a week. I make sure that she's long gone before James arrives. I wouldn't want him to think that anyone else was preparing his chocolate treats for him. Perhaps Martha's got a friend who'd like a few hours of extra work.

My business isn't the only thing that's expanding.

'Do you think I'm getting fat?' James asks as he devours a large slice of my mocha and coconut cake with its thick, coffee-butter icing and pieces of chocolate flake on top. I think this will go down very well with my customers.

'Do you?' he says again.

'What?'

'Think that I'm getting fat.'

The hollows of his cheeks have filled out to plump little apples and there's a softening around his waist.

'No,' I say, loyally.

He smoothes his hands down the burgeoning curve of his stomach. 'Claire thinks that I'm getting a bit too chubby.'

'She said that?'

'Yes.' James turns doleful eyes towards me.

'Really?'

His little paunch sits over the waistband of his jeans. 'She's trying to put me on a diet.'

'How awful,' I commiserate. 'Does she know that you come to see me every night?'

James flushes. 'No,' he says. 'That's our little secret.'

'And so it shall remain,' I tell him as, with a warm smile, I slide a tray of chocolate walnut squares from the oven. 'More cake?'

Emily, my new assistant, comes to collect the keys for the van and load up for the day. There's chocolate tray bake, caramel shortbread, chocolate lemon tarts and cappuccino fancies to name but a few of the delights on offer. We stack them up and trail downstairs to the lock-up garages that house the two Chocoholics Anonymous vans.

I had some details from the estate agent's this morning through the post. It's time that I moved out of the flat and into somewhere bigger. I'm looking for a house, perhaps with a place that I could park the vans that doesn't involve three flights of stairs. Maybe somewhere that I could get a small industrial unit nearby. It would have to be somewhere easily accessible for Martha and Dorothy, my two cooks, as I couldn't manage without them both. Chocoholics Anonymous has now got a website and we take our vans to private parties, festivals and even onto film locations. I could really do with another couple of vans to keep up with demand.

'Claire's left me,' James says miserably, as he helps himself to yet another one of my chocolate macaroons.

'I'm sorry to hear that,' I say, taking a bowl of melted chocolate from the top of the cooker.

'These are delicious. I can't get enough of them.' James checks out one more. There are chocolate and coconut crumbs on his lips. 'She said I'd let myself go.'

'The diet didn't work?'

James moves onto the plate of chocolate and ginger Florentines. 'These things never do, do they? Who can live on lettuce alone?'

'No one,' I sympathise.

While I drizzle dark chocolate over my chocolate and hazelnut cookies, I take a good long look at James's face. The lean, handsome features have all but disappeared. The plump apple cheeks have blossomed. James's chiselled jaw now carries more chins than the Chinese phone book. The little barrel of his stomach rests comfortably on his thighs. Is that a hint of man-boobs I can see?

'I should never have left you,' my ex-boyfriend and Claire's ex-boyfriend continues. 'You always looked after me so well. I don't know what got into me. I was hasty. Foolish.'

'We all do things we regret,' I say. 'Try these.' I push a tray of fruit and nut refrigerator fingers towards him. They're gooey concoctions of mixed fruit, hazelnuts, digestive biscuits and marshmallow hanging together in rich, dark chocolate. I take a piece myself. James and I eat together.

'Good,' he says with a contented nod. 'Very good.' He demolishes another calorie-laden finger or two just to be sure. 'Now that Claire's gone, perhaps we could spend more time together. Get back to how we were.'

Next, I think I'll make some chocolate pecan pie – that's always very popular with my customers.

'What do you say?' James looks at me hopefully. It's an expression that has been on my face for so long that it seems strange to see my ex-lover wearing it. There's chocolate round his mouth and crumbs down the front of his shirt.

'I don't think so,' I tell him. 'I'm moving out of the flat. I've bought a new home and I'm leasing a small business unit so that I can increase production. I'll be gone soon.'

'But you can't go.' James looks panic-stricken. 'What will

I do? I come here every night. How will I manage without you?'

I break a bar of rich, dark chocolate into tiny pieces and smile at James. 'You can have *too* much of a good thing, you know.'

Christmas Stories

To be honest, I was never the biggest fan of Christmas until I started writing and reading seasonal books. But now I find that thinking about mince pies and mistletoe in July really gets me in the mood for Christmas nice and early. I fully embrace it all and can't wait until it comes round. Yes, I confess that I'm one of those who are deliriously happy when the Christmas cards hit the shops in August! I try to get Lovely Kev to put the Christmas tree up earlier and earlier. A couple of years ago, my mum was ill over Christmas and so we had a delayed Christmas in February. I left my tree up until we'd celebrated properly and I did consider leaving it up all year. It hardly seemed worth putting it back in the loft by then. Unfortunately, Lovely Kev wasn't quite so enamoured with the idea.

Even if you're reading these with the sun blazing down, I hope the next four stories will put a little winter warmth into your heart and get you dreaming about Christmas.

Sunshine with a Chance of Snow

July

We've saved up for this holiday for so long that I can still hardly believe that we're actually here. The St Lucian sun is blazing down, the sun lounger is set at the perfect angle to catch all of the rays. My colourful cocktail replete with pretty paper umbrella is on a table at my side, so close to hand that I don't even have to reach out – just as a drink should be. The book I'm reading is as scorching hot as the sun.

I let my arm drop and trail my hand in the white sand, letting the grains run through my fingers. The soothing sound of the waves lapping against the shore threatens to make my novel redundant as my eyes grow heavy. I can't think of a time when I've felt more relaxed. All I have to do is ring a little bell on the table and a lovely waiter comes running to see if I need a freshener. Bliss. This is what life is about.

Turning to Michael who's on the lounger right next to me, I say, 'This is heaven, isn't it?'

'Paradise.' He opens he eyes and gazes at me. 'It's been hard work getting here, Beth, but I'm glad you pushed for us to do it.'

'Me too.'

My husband of ten years is still a handsome man. I fell in love the moment I saw him. He was playing football for a local team and I'd been dragged along by my friend whose boyfriend was also in the team. I thought it was the dullest thing I'd ever seen, yet I couldn't take my eyes off the man with a mop of dark hair who had very nice legs. I can't even remember what the score was or which side won. We met in the bar afterward when he was freshly showered, but still looking tousled. He smiled and the room and my heart lit up. His eyes, which I now know are the colour of the Caribbean Sea and filled with fun, locked on mine. He had me even before he said, 'Hello'. But once I heard his dark brown voice, that was me gone. My fate sealed.

We dated briefly and married quickly. A budget wedding at the local register office, two days in Brighton in lieu of a honeymoon. We've promised ourselves for so long that we would go somewhere special yet there was something else to think about, something else to pay for. Neither of us earns mega-bucks and money – or lack of it – is a constant issue. Yet now we're here. On honeymoon, ten years too late, with two kids in tow.

I haven't stopped loving Michael for a second in all that time. Not that we haven't had our ups and downs. Bringing up children these days is always going to be a challenge, isn't it? And we're blessed with two of the completely hyperactive variety. Jess is eight now and Kade is coming up to six. They're a handful, there's no denying it – what kids aren't? They're on the go morning, noon and night. I can't remember when Michael and I last had some quality time together as a couple. It takes us all our time to keep up with their rota of activities. You've got to do it now, haven't you? A plethora of clubs, societies and outings to turn them into rounded citizens. In my day, if you were lucky, you either did ballet or piano lessons – end of. These two have busier social lives than we do. It all costs a fortune too. But I want them to have everything in life that we didn't and if that means sacrifice then so be it. We work our socks off to give them all that we can. But we both love them to bits and wouldn't have it any other way.

This is the first time we've all been abroad together as a family. Before Michael and I met, when we were still young and single, we had a few holidays abroad. I went to Spain with the girls for a week. Nowhere exotic. Michael had been on a few rugby club trips – France, Holland, and the like. Since we had the kids, cash has always been tight. When we can afford a holiday, we usually go camping with them to the Lake District, Wales or Cornwall. But I feel as if the kids are missing out. All of their friends go abroad – some of them twice a year. I see my friend's pictures on Facebook and I want that for us too. So this year we went for it and decided to treat ourselves to a bit of luxury. You can't always be the ones who have to make do and mend.

I've been working part-time up until recently – just school hours in an office doing a bit of accounts work – as I like to be around for the kids. So that we could save for this holiday, I've gone full-time. I work until half past five every day, often later. The kids now go into an after-school club or sometimes to a child minder who lives a couple of streets away. It eats up a fair bit of the extra money, but she's brilliant and will supervise their homework or will give them their tea, so they can go straight to bed when either Michael or I pick them up.

I wish my family were nearer and they could help more. But we wanted a bigger house and so had to move away from them to a cheaper area. It takes about an hour to drive there, so they're not always on hand, and now that we're so busy, we've seen less of them. Mum complains, but it can't be helped.

Michael's worked extra hours too and we've stashed all the extra overtime pay away, resisting the temptation to blow it on fripperies such as a new carpet to replace the dog-eared one in the dining room. The house needs total redecorating really. We could only afford this place as it needs a facelift. 'Much loved,' Michael calls it when he really means falling down round our ears. We'd need a lottery win to sort it.

The danger now is that all the time we're anxious about the future. It's hard not to be. Michael's job is never one hundred per cent secure and it's always at the back of your mind about what will happen tomorrow. What if he loses his job? What if we can't pay the bills? I can't think of anything worse and yet it's a constant threat. We always seem to be stressed out.

My mum thinks we're putting ourselves under even more pressure by jetting off like this. But I think that's why it's good for us to have this break together. I booked the first plane that I could at the end of the kids' school term. We've worked our backsides off for it, but I think it's worth it. Sometimes it's all too easy to concentrate on the mundane and not stop to look at the stars. You have to think big if you want to get on, don't you?

A breeze from the ocean wafts over us. The palm trees rustle.

'If I died now,' Michael sighs, 'I would die a happy man.'

The wind makes me shiver and goose bumps rise on my arms. 'Don't say that,' I chide. 'It sounds like tempting fate.'

'We'll live to a ripe old age,' he promises me. 'All that broccoli you've force fed me over the years has assured it.'

'We might stand a chance of reaching ninety if we learn to relax or can take a holiday like this every now and then.'

'It's been a hard year,' Michael agrees. 'I feel like we've hardly seen the kids. Or each other.'

'You've got to do it if you want the nice things in life.'

It's good to experience the warmth on my skin. I've been so tired recently and the flight was a killer. Nine hours on a cramped plane to get to the Caribbean. The sun feels as if it's strengthening my bones, my muscles. It's so different to when you're at home in England and it's sunny and you're having to work,

work, work. When I'm not working I'm ironing or cooking. I'm sure there's another family who dumps their washing in our house too. If you can't be lying on a sun lounger in it, then the heat is just annoying. It's all I can do to grab an hour in the garden with my book at the weekends.

'I could fancy coming here again. Maybe one Christmas,' Michael says. 'Do something a bit different for a change.'

'No.' I'm horrified. 'Any other time of the year. I love Christmas at home. We couldn't go away. It just wouldn't be the same.'

If I'm honest with you, we also had to dip into the Christmas fund for spending money for this trip. So it's sadly depleted now. Now it's my turn to sigh.

'Christmas will have to be low-key this year,' Michael warns as if he's reading my mind. 'There's no way we'll be able to do our usual thing.'

I confess that the festive season is my favourite time of the year. I've adored it since I was a child and love to make it idyllic for my own children. The minute the first snow falls we're out playing in it. I can still think of nothing I like to do more than to spend an hour building a snowman or getting the sledges out and finding the nearest snowy slope. Our home is always filled with decorations and we have the most enormous real tree. Michael says that it looks like Santa's grotto and pretends that he does Christmas under sufferance but, secretly, I think he likes it too.

We have all the family round – Mum, Dad, my brother, Paul, and sister, Karen. Michael's family joins us too, so the house is crammed. The table groans with food and I do like to go a bit mad with presents, but everything is special and chosen with love. I spend all year looking for that perfect thing for everyone. And, of course, the kids like all the latest toys.

'We'll never save up again in time, Beth.' Michael frowns and I don't want him doing that on a Caribbean beach. 'The kids will have to understand that this holiday has been their main treat. I'll just get a few bits and bobs for them. But it will still be fun.'

For the first time ever, I think it would be much better if we could put Christmas back by six months. 'You have to do Christmas properly,' I cajole. 'Otherwise it's just not right.'

'We have to cut our cloth accordingly,' he tells me. 'We'll do what we can to make it special, but it won't be our usual extravagance. Though I bet you still make me go up into the loft to get down all the Christmas tat that we've got stashed up there.'

'You can count on it.'

Michael laughs. 'I can't believe that we're talking about Christmas in July.'

'You know me; Christmas can never come quickly enough.' I even have an app on my phone to count down the days.

'I'm serious, Beth. This year we can't do it.'

I grin at him. I've got months to talk Michael round and perhaps we can both do some extra hours at work when we get back. 'It will be wonderful. You wait and see.'

The children race up to us, scattering sand in their wake. We made sure that we booked them into the kid's club so that we could have some time to ourselves. There's no point having palm trees and deserted beaches if you don't have a minute's peace and quiet to go with them. But it is lovely to have some quality time together as a family. We do so much racing around at home that we're very rarely all in the same room together.

Jess throws herself into my arms, knocking my book for six. 'We're having a quick break for some juice,' she says, breathlessly. 'So we thought we'd come to see you.'

'That's nice.' I look at her shoulders. 'You're going a bit pink. This sun is stronger than we're used to. Pass me that sunscreen.'

89

She does as she's told and I rub in some more cream. Kade has been having tennis lessons while Jess is trying out a bit of snorkelling. I want them to experience all that they can while they're here. And they've loved every minute of it. This also means that we get to enjoy them when they've run off all their energy.

Jess lies down next to me and I smooth her fringe from her forehead before I wrap my arms around her. She looks like me with long, dark hair that will never be tamed by straighteners. My daughter's long-limbed and will be a knock-out one day. Kade is the spitting image of Michael. His father's son. He's sturdy, big-boned. He's already playing rugby for the local junior team, which scares the life out of me. I can't stand seeing my baby knocked flat to the ground by the bigger boys.

'Having fun this afternoon?' Michael asks.

Kade nods, fidgeting now he's had to sit still for more than a second.

'How's the tennis going?' Michael wants to know. 'Going to become the next Roger Federer and keep your old man in the style he's becoming accustomed to?'

'What?' Kade says.

Michael lowers his sunglasses and says to me. 'A long way to go yet.'

'Come and play with me later, Dad?'

'Yeah,' Michael says. 'But first we have to have a siesta, sleep off our lunch. It's the law out here.'

'You're sad,' Kade tells him.

'Sad and old,' I agree.

'Got to go. Things to do,' Jess says. 'Laters.'

We laugh as we watch them speed off again, running along the white beach, kicking up sand in their wake.

'Laters,' Michael echoes, mimicking Jess.

She'll be a teenager before we know it and then we'll have our hands full.

My husband shifts in his sun lounger, turning towards me. 'How long before the kids are back from their club again?'

I check my watch. 'Another hour or more.'

'We could go and have our customary little lie down together in our beautiful, air-conditioned room.'

In the few days that we've been here, we've already fallen into the habit of sneaking away in the afternoon and making love while the kids are otherwise occupied. Something else to recommend a luxury holiday rather than camping. At home we fall in to bed every night exhausted and it's the last thing on our minds. But here with the warm days and sultry nights, our passion is rising again.

'We could,' I agree as I wiggle my eyebrows in a seductive manner. I dieted like mad for this holiday. There was no way I wanted to be waddling along the beach, wrapped up in a sarong. I'm pleased I did as I think my old man is fancying me in my bikini, which is perhaps a bit skimpy for a mother of two who's pushing forty.

So, like naughty teenagers, we gather up our belongings and hurry back to our room. It's decorated perfectly for romance. There are two large French windows, which open out onto a balcony that overlooks the sparkling, blue Caribbean ocean. Gossamer drapes flutter in the breeze. Everything is cool and painted white. The bed, which is dressed with crisp, white sheets. If only I could get my bedding to look like this at home.

I stroke Michael's face as he kicks off his shorts. His face is pink from the sun, faint freckles dust his nose. A tan suits him.

He undoes my bikini top and, jokingly, he throws it onto the ceiling fan that whirrs slowly above us. We giggle together, and then his fingers gently trace the tan lines that contour my breasts.

'Still beautiful,' he breathes.

Then, he scoops me up into his arms and twirls me round.

91

'Michael!'

He leaps onto the bed, throwing us both down with a bounce. Even now, when we get the chance, we like a bit of rough and tumble.

'Sssh.' I laugh out loud. 'Someone will hear.'

'Let them.'

But, as we turn together and I sink into his arms, I get a sharp pain in the side of my breast. 'Ouch.' I cup myself.

'Are you OK?' Michael frowns with concern. 'Did I hurt you?'

'I don't know,' I tell him. 'I'm really tender.'

'It's probably all that swimming you've been doing. I bet you've used muscles that haven't seen the light of day for years.'

'I expect you're right.'

His finger circles my nipple. 'I'll be gentle with you,' he teases. 'I promise.'

'I'm sure it's nothing.'

But as I touch my breast I feel a lump. It's hard, palpable and I'm pretty certain that it wasn't there before.

December

The light is bright on my eyes and I struggle against the heaviness of the lids. I wish I was wearing sunglasses to cut the glare, but I don't think I could bear the weight on my face. I feel leaden in the bed and the wires that run in and out of my limbs make me feel as if I'm pinned down just like Gulliver was in Lilliput. A warm kiss on my forehead and a hand stroking my hair gives me the final impetus to open my tired eyes. 'Michael?'

My mouth is dry, in need of a drink. Instinctively, my husband lifts a glass to my lips. The water is warm, dusty and has the chemical tang of bleach. 'Merry Christmas, darling.'

'Is it Christmas Day?' I hadn't realised. Since I've been in here, the days have all blurred into one. I've done nothing but sleep and yet I'm still so exhausted.

He nods. 'Not much of a celebration this year.'

'No.' I turn and the sticking plaster below my Hickman Line pulls at the skin on my chest.

'How are you feeling today?'

'I'm fine.' I'm sick from the chemo and weary of lying in this hospital bed. I'd hoped to be home for Christmas but, well, life never works out quite how you plan it.

Michael looks tired, pale. There's no trace of his golden, St Lucian suntan now. That and the sprinkling of freckles it left on his nose are long gone. Our Caribbean holiday seems like a world away.

It's been hard for Michael holding everything together while I've been having treatment for the cancerous tumour in my breast. He's had to work, ferry the children around and then has raced back here every night for visiting time. It's a punishing routine. My parents have been fantastic. They were trailing backwards and forward every day to help out but it was too much for them. So now Mum and Dad have both moved into our place. It's more than a bit squashed, but they've taken over the day-to-day care of the children while Michael goes out to work, and they have also done the afternoon shift of visiting me. They've done a sterling job. I don't know how we would have coped without them.

I reach up and touch my husband's face. I want to feel him, look at him as much as I can. I'm frightened that, despite all these monitors, the nurses bustling around, that I'll slip quietly away in the night and no one will notice.

'I'll see if I can find a nurse to get some fresh water.' He puts down my glass. Next to it there's a picture of us all on holiday, something to remind me of better times, to bring warmth and to brighten the clinical ward. I look at us, all smiles, posing beneath the palm trees, the sparkling sea behind us and think that you never know what's waiting for you just around the corner.

'Don't leave me,' I say. 'Not yet.'

To think that a few months ago, on the holiday that I discovered my lump, we had a little bell just to summon a waiter. All I was worried about was choosing which cocktail I'd like from the extensive menu. Now look at me. I look like someone else in the photo. I hardly recognise myself. If I'm honest, I don't think I'm that person now.

Michael sits down in the chair next to the bed. It looks terribly uncomfortable but he never complains, though he's spent hours perched in it. He holds my hand tenderly as if he's afraid that I might break. Absently, his thumb gently strokes the reddened skin around the cannula that comes out of the back.

'How are Jess and Kade?' I ask.

'Bearing up,' he says. 'They're waiting outside with your mum. I thought I'd have you to myself for a few minutes before the onslaught.'

'I miss them.' A tear slides out of my eye and runs down my cheek. Michael takes a tissue from the box in my bedside cabinet, which is stacked with the accoutrements of sickness and dabs it away.

'They miss you too.'

I'm only allowed a few visitors due to the risk of them bringing in an infection and the children have only been to see me a few times, which is so very difficult. My mum and dad do their daily duty. Karen and Paul have been along too with their partners. My friends have been fantastic as well, but they're all on a strictly controlled rota so that I'm not overwhelmed.

'I expect Mum's got the dinner going already?'

'Yes.' Michael nods. I'm worried about how weary he looks.

'Your dad's been on potato peeling since dawn. We're going to eat later this afternoon when we get back from here. It'll just be quiet. It won't be the same without you.' His eyes fill with unshed tears. The last time I saw Michael cry was when Kade was born.

I think of the things we normally do at Christmas and my heart could break.

'I feel as if I'm letting the children down.' I thought that our only worry this year would be that money would be tight. I never in my worst nightmares envisaged this.

'Don't be silly,' Michael says. 'They know why we're not having our usual celebration. All they want is their mum to be better again.'

All my resolution to be strong disappears and I cry in Michael's arms, letting him cradle me like a child.

'Dry your eyes.' He finds another tissue. 'You'll ruin your mascara.'

That makes me laugh as the last of my eyelashes fell out last week as well he knows.

'They understand,' he says. 'They're growing up fast.'

And I hope with all of my heart that I'll be there to see it.

'I'll go and get them both,' he says. 'That'll cheer you up.'

He props me up on the pillows so that I'm sitting more upright, even the exertion of that makes me exhausted. Who knew that the small, hard lump that I found in my breast would prove to be so troublesome and tenacious. I run my hand through my sparse hair to tidy myself up and more wisps come away in my fingers. My hair has always driven me mad. I've cursed its frizzy wantonness. Now I'm fearful of its loss.

Michael constantly reminds me of all the beautiful baldies there have been: Sinead O'Connor, Gail Porter and, his favourite one of all, Sigourney Weaver as Ripley in *Aliens*. He says he doesn't care if I'm blonde, brunette or bald as long as I'm still here. I'm trying to oblige him and the doctors tell me that my prognosis is good. The gruelling rounds of chemotherapy shrank the tumour as it was supposed to. The subsequent surgery, they say, has been very successful. I guess the acid test of that will be if I'm still alive and kicking in twenty years' time.

Jess and Kade walk carefully down the ward, anxious not to disturb the other dozing patients in the few occupied beds. All the patients who were capable were sent home for Christmas. But not me. As soon as Jess and Kade get near to me, they can't contain themselves and run to my side.

I hug them as tightly as I can. I don't care if I feel it jarring down to my bones, I just want to feel their solidity against me, fill my nostrils with the scent of children instead of medicine.

'We've asked Santa to make you better,' Jess says when I finally let her go.

'Then I'm sure I'll be just fine.'

Her eyes sparkle with tears.

'No crying,' I say. 'It's Christmas Day.'

'It's horrible without you.'

'I'll be home soon enough,' I tell her. 'This year we have to make the best of it.'

'We put the tree up last night,' she says. 'Dad got that old, manky fake one out of the loft.'

'Does it look good?'

'No.' She shakes her head. 'It's not the same as when you do it. Grandma did most of it, but she's rubbish at it.'

'I'm sure it looks lovely.'

'Kade broke the head off the fairy.'

'I didn't mean to,' he flares.

'It doesn't matter. We'll get another one for next year.'

'We've got a star on it,' Jess complains. 'It looks well stupid.'

I'm just glad that Mum has done something even if it doesn't meet with Jess's exacting standards. Michael simply hasn't had time to do anything as he's been running around so much. I don't think he could face the enforced jollity either, though he's putting a brave face on it for the kids.

For me, it will be as if Christmas doesn't exist this year.

The ward isn't decorated either. The nurses said that they used to try to pretty things up with a bit of tinsel and a fake tree but, apparently, Health and Safety put paid to that sort of thing years ago. There's a Christmas dinner served but as I'm not keeping any food down, that doesn't really matter to me. I also think that the Salvation Army comes in and there'll be some Christmas carols later.

A few minutes later, Mum scurries down the ward. She comes forward and I kiss her too.

'I've brought you some of my mince pies.' Mum shuffles everything about on the bedside cabinet so that she can put down the Tupperware container she's clutching. 'Still warm.'

It's obviously slipped her mind that I can't yet eat properly. But my mum bakes great mince pies and the nurses will love them.

'The turkey's in. I've left your dad in charge.' She rolls her eyes at that. 'But it will be hours yet. I can plate you some up for when we come back later.'

'Don't really feel like it,' I confess. I clutch her hand and squeeze. She feels as frail as me. This has been a trial for her too. I wonder how I'd feel if it was Jess lying here and I was the one visiting. 'We couldn't manage without you. Thanks for looking after them all.'

She squeezes back, but she can't answer me as she's too choked.

I cuddle the children to me. Kade, unusually quiet, says very little. I think he's inherited his dad's loathing for hospitals.

Out of the window, a few flakes of snow start to fall. 'Look,' I say. 'It's going to be a white Christmas.'

'We'd normally get the sledges out,' Jess says, 'and build a snowman.'

'You can still do that,' I assure them. 'If it sticks, Dad will take you out later.'

'Of course, I will,' Michael says, but his voice is gruff and his eyes are too bright.

'Come home soon, Mummy,' Kade says, leaning against me. 'We need you. Christmas isn't the same without you.'

'I'll do my very best,' I promise.

I pull them towards me and hold them tight. They lie down beside me on the bed even though they're not supposed to. Michael's right. They're growing up fast and I so desperately want to be there to see it. I want to see Jess blossom into a beautiful woman. I want to see Kade as a man every bit as handsome as his dad. I want to see them both married with children. More than anything, I want to be here. I want to grow old.

A nurse comes along pushing the drugs trolley. 'Merry Christmas, everyone,' she says brightly. 'Your mum will be home with you soon. Don't you worry. That'll be a nice Christmas present at any time of the year.'

As she counts out my tablets, I look out of the window and watch the meandering flakes. For once I'm not dreaming of a white Christmas; I'm just dreaming of seeing another Christmas at all.

July

Sitting in a deckchair in the garden, I catch some early morning sunshine. Summer in England has started late this year, but it's finally here and I'm grateful for it. If I'm honest, it's probably a bit too cool for sitting out yet, but I want to make the most of every single ray. I thank God for every sunny day that I see.

My small, scrubby patch of garden, which never gets enough attention, now seems to me like the best place on earth.

The blossoming of spring coincided with my hair re-growing on my head and now I'm sporting a short, funky style that looks as if it's been done quite by intention rather than the aggressiveness of medicine. Michael says that I look years younger. And I feel good, really good.

I think I'm nearly at the end of my dance with cancer and then, even though I have to take drugs for the foreseeable future, all in my world will be well. So long as I take life at a more sedate pace than I used to. I lost my job while I was ill. The bouquet from my colleagues arrived on the same day as the letter from Human Resources dropped on the mat that said my services would no longer be required. I don't feel up to looking for another job just yet, but I'll find something else again when I'm ready. Something part-time. Nothing too taxing. But, for now, I'm just happy to be at home.

We put ourselves under too much strain last year. I can see that now. Of course, I can. But it's so easy to do. Like so many people, I got caught up in all the hype about what you 'must have' these days. Now I know what really matters. Cancer pulls you up short. When you're faced with the possibility that you *won't* live, it really makes you stop and think about how you *do* live.

Nice as it was, there'll be no more slaving away to afford a big holiday abroad. I know now that I can get as much pleasure in the bright yellow cheeriness of a few daffodils or watching the fat bees buzz round the roses as I can with palm trees and white sand. Watching the sunset from my bedroom window is just as impressive as it is in the Caribbean. The other thing I learned is that as long as you're surrounded by your loved ones, then it doesn't really matter where you are.

I must confess though, the only thing I really missed was Christmas as it went largely unmarked last year. Most of my time was spent asleep or out of it on drugs. Neither of which are conducive to the festive spirit. It's not right to have a year without Christmas and it seems so long until the next one. But even that will be scaled back from now on. A family doesn't need a heap of presents under the tree to show how much they love each other. I know how much they love me from the hours they spent at my hospital bedside, drawn and hollowed-eyed, willing me to get well again.

So now, while I'm on the mend, I just want to be at home with the family and take every day as it comes. I want Michael to cut back on his work too. For months he looked so drained and grey with all the time he spent at the hospital, but now his colour is returning too. There'll be no more overtime just to afford the latest phones, laptops or all the other nonsense we don't need. All the kids really want is for us to be here for them. They've stopped a lot of their after school activities too. I've realised that they don't have to be on the go all the time to be happy either. I'd rather we were all just around the house, spending time together. If we live with crappy dining room carpet for the rest of our lives, then so be it.

Kade is playing in the sandpit at the bottom of the garden and Michael is doing whatever men do in their sheds. Jess comes out of the house with a cup of tea for me. As well as newly discovered tea-making skills, she also now makes her own bed every day without being asked and she'll even run the hoover round if pressed.

'That's very kind, sweetheart,' I say, taking the milky tea. I put it to one side and pull her onto my knee for a cuddle.

'Nana was on the phone,' she tells me. 'She says will you go to the shops with her for a couple of hours?'

'Of course, I will. Do I need to ring her back?'

'No,' Jess says. 'She's coming round.'

Mum and Dad have moved back home now, but their house

has been sold and they've had an offer accepted on a little bungalow that's only five minutes away. I can't wait for the move to go through as I want them round the corner from me again as soon as possible.

'I'll have my tea and get ready. Want to come with us?'

'No,' she says. 'I'll stay here with Daddy.'

'You're turning down an opportunity to shop?' Normally, she's first in the car when that's on offer.

'I don't need anything.' But there's a strange glint in her eyes when she says, 'I have things to do.'

A date with MSN, no doubt. Things are obviously getting back to normal in our household.

For the first few weeks when I came out of hospital, Jess wouldn't let me out of her sight. We've become closer as mother and daughter. As well as her helping around the house, we bake together, read together, sit and watch rubbish telly side by side. Perhaps she can now relax again as I've been around for a while and it doesn't look as if I'm going anywhere in a hurry.

My child is growing up and, all the time I was ill, I worried that I'd wouldn't be here to see her blossom into a young woman, wouldn't be there to comfort her when her heart was first broken, wouldn't see her as a bride. Perhaps I can start to relax now too.

My mum comes and she fusses around me, still treating me as if I'm made of china. Our relationship has changed too and not a day goes by when I don't see her. So often the only things that you need are right in front of you all the time. It's all very nice striving for holidays abroad, the latest television or phone, but that's not what it's about, is it? If there's any silver lining from my brush with cancer, it's that I know that now. It's written indelibly on my heart.

'Didn't Karen fancy coming with us too?'

'Busy,' Mum says, but doesn't offer any further enlightenment.

I've seen more of my sister and brother recently too. It's easy to drift apart without really meaning to and it's sad that it takes a life-threatening illness to bring us all together again.

Michael appears from the shed, where he's clearly been very industrious as I haven't seen him all morning.

'I've only got to get a few things,' Mum says as we make to leave for our impromptu shopping expedition.

'Take care of her,' he instructs. 'Don't keep her out for too long and remember to have a coffee break.'

'We'll be back in two hours,' Mum replies, giving Michael what my dad calls the 'look'. 'No longer.'

'Sure you don't want to come?' I give Jess another chance to change her mind.

She shakes her head and stands side by side with her father. 'Laters,' she says.

So Mum and I go shopping alone. We take it at a steady pace and it's still unnerving that I tire more easily than my parents now. Mum picks up the bits that she needs and we have a mooch, but I find the Saturday crowds overwhelming. So, as Michael has instructed, we find a café that's not so rammed and tuck ourselves into the corner. Mum goes to the counter to get the coffees and a piece of cake for each of us.

We sit and chat about nothing in particular, but I can tell that she's twitchy today.

'Anything wrong?'

'No, no.' Then she checks her watch. 'Oh, look at the time,' she says. 'We'd better get back.'

'I'm in no hurry.'

'I promised Michael we'd be back. I'd better text him.'

'He won't mind. He's quite happy in his shed. I've left instructions for lunch with Jess. They'll be fine.'

'Come on, Beth. Look lively.' Mum's tiding the cups, chivvying me up. Clearly my words have fallen on deaf ears. She downs her coffee and taps a text into her phone as her grandchildren have shown her. (Use thumbs, Grandma!)

On the way home, my mother drives at breakneck speed.

'Where's the fire?' I ask.

'It's because you're not used to being a passenger,' she says as we career around yet another corner.

When we turn into our road, I'm mightily relieved to get home without a ticket from the boys in blue.

'Well . . .' Mum adjusts her hair as she climbs out of the car. 'Here we are.'

Here we are, indeed. I feel as if I've been on a test drive with Jensen Button.

I put my key in the lock. 'Staying for a cuppa?'

'Oh,' she says. 'Go on then. Just a quick one. Your father will wonder where I've got to.'

When I open the living room door, I'm stunned at the sight that greets me. Michael, Jess and Kade stand together grinning at me as my mouth gapes open. They've certainly been busy since I've been out.

'Merry Christmas,' Michael says.

Despite it being July, a real Christmas tree towers in the corner of the room, beautifully bedecked with all the baubles that mean so much to me. The lights shine out boldly on this bright, summer day. And, just as I would normally do, the mantelpiece is dressed with ivy and bows. The Christmas cards that we received when I was in hospital, the ones that I missed, are all out on display. Everything has been replicated to perfection from my favourite season of the year.

'Wow.'

Jess and Kade run to hug me.

'Do you like it, Mummy?' Kade asks anxiously. 'We worked very hard with Daddy while you were out.'

'It's fantastic.' I can't stop the tears now. 'Just fantastic.'

Then the dining room door slides open and there's my dear dad. My sister and brother, along with their families, are right behind him. The table is all set complete with red tablecloth. My very best Christmas crockery is out in force. The glass and gold glitters in the sunshine. There are even crackers.

'Dinner won't be long,' Dad says, his voice thick with emotion.

'Don't tell me that you've cooked a Christmas dinner too?'

'With all the trimmings,' my sister adds as she hugs me. 'I did the turkey and brought it round with me. Merry Christmas, Beth.'

I turn to my brother, Paul. 'You were in on this too?'

'Sorry, sis.' But his grin says that he's not sorry at all.

I look over at Michael. 'How did you do all this without me knowing?'

'With a lot of hard work and skulduggery. I've made liars out of all your family.'

'You have!' I turn to my speed freak mother. 'I wondered why you were in such a rush to get back. Now I know.'

'Michael would have lynched me if I'd been late.'

'I could have brought some Christmas presents while we were out,' I tease.

'No presents,' Michael says. 'You're the only gift that we need.'

And, of course, that makes me cry.

'Come on,' Mum says. 'Let's have lunch.' She ushers everyone through to the dining room.

Michael and I stay back for a moment on our own.

'Thank you so much for this.'

'I know that you love Christmas. I hated that you missed one. Now that you're well on the road to recovery, I thought that you deserved a special treat.'

'I can't believe that you managed to keep it from me,' I tell him. 'But I'm glad that you did.'

He holds me tightly. 'At one point, I was terrified that we might never have another Christmas together, Beth.'

'Me too.'

'It's been a terrible year.'

'It has. But I feel that it's taught me a lot too.' I might have battle scars to show for my struggle, but I also feel that something in my soul has settled. I no longer feel the need to strive to get the bigger, better, brighter things. I thought I was doing a good thing in wanting to give the children everything I could, but all they really want is for me to be here. 'All that's important to me is my family and being around for you.' I reach up and kiss my husband. 'We *will* grow old together.'

'I'll hold you to that,' he says. Then he holds some mistletoe that he happens to have handy above our heads and kisses me until my head swims.

'Dinner's getting cold!' 'Mum shouts. 'Chop, chop.'

So we go into the dining room and join our family. Wizzard are singing 'I Wish it Could be Christmas Everyday.' We all pull crackers and put on our festive hats. I throw open the patio doors and we eat a lovely festive lunch in the warm, summer sunshine. No chance of a white Christmas today. But it hardly matters as I bathe in the love and laughter that surrounds me.

I lift my glass high and propose a toast.

'To family and to the future. To health and happiness,' I say as the champagne sparkles. 'And to many, many more Christmases to come.'

All I Want for Christmas is You

It's the first day of December. The start of Advent. That delicious period of excitement leading up to the joyous frenzy that is Christmas. Unless, of course, you're without a man and then it's a pants time of dodging unwanted and embarrassing invitations simply because when they say 'Maria Plus One', you've got no lovely 'Plus One' stylee boyfriend to go along with.

And I can be sure that from now until New Year, at every seasonal family gathering my crusty old relations, who have been dredged up for their annual airing, will say in very loud voices, 'Not married yet then, Maria?' or 'Still no Mr Right, Love?' or words to that effect. It's the same every year and I have to make sure that there are no sharp objects in my handbag to stab them with or stale mince pies to hand to throw at them.

Chrissie and I sigh at each other over our skimmed milk lattes – the ones that Chrissie just nipped out to get from the new coffee bar across the road from the office – Coffee Café.

Our depression has been brought on due to the fact that we've both realised that the office Christmas party is looming large once more.

'This is the third year that we'll both be without a man,' I say, sinking lower to my desk.

The comment was rather unnecessary as we are both more than aware of our single status. And the great myth about singledom is that it's fun. Oh, yeah. Sitting at home alone over

Christmas with a box of 'Eat Me' dates – the only dates I'm likely to get. A barrel of laughs.

'Do you think if I write to Santa and ask for a man he'll oblige?' I ask my friend.

I let myself daydream. Dear Santa, I'd like a tall, dark handsome stranger please. Doesn't have to be too rich, too bright or even too handsome. The nearest manly specimen he has lying around unused on his dusty little Santa shelves will do just fine.

'No,' Chrissie says firmly. 'Last year I asked for a pair of Manolo Blahniks and I got a pair of Marks & Spencer's fluffy slippers instead. Santa is useless, Maria. Live with it.'

At least I did get a new car last year. A gorgeous, festively red little number, complete with all the bells and whistles a girl could ever want. I did have to buy it myself, of course. It wasn't waiting on my doorstep with a bow tied round it bought by my millionaire toy-boy lover who couldn't decide between that and a small yacht.

Still, you can't have everything in life. I let my eyes rove out to the car park where my lovely car is sitting waiting patiently to whisk me away from the drudgery that is my working day. My eyes then go to my watch – my moment of escape is hours away yet. I sigh again.

'Eyes right,' Chrissie hisses under her breath and my gaze swivels again.

We have a new hunk in the office. The *only* hunk in the office. Chrissie and I work as Editorial Assistants at a very small publishing house. Think the smallest publishing house you can imagine. Our books are earnest self-help tomes bought by the sort of women who think tofu is a marvellous foodstuff. We have a handful of middle-aged editors who all wear kaftans or ethnic knits and have their hair dyed in varying shades of aubergine. There's a Managing Director who wears a white linen suit, a tie with dollar signs all over it and red socks. He also carries a raffia shopping bag. Everyone in the marketing department is over fifty and bald.

And now we have Lovely Richard. Well-cut suit, gelled, spiky hair, expensive shoes. He is the future of Earth Publishing. Lovely Richard has been head-hunted from a proper publishing company and brought in by our despairing owner to widen our acquisitions – i.e. books that don't feature vegetables, vegan clothing and Reiki quite as heavily.

Chrissie is in love with Richard. She thinks it's because he's adorably handsome and charming. I think it's because we are very bored and have small lives and, therefore, are easily swayed.

Richard stops by our desks. He does this a lot.

'Hey,' he says. 'What's new?'

There is never anything new at Earth Publishing and we remind him of this constantly. He assures us this will change and that, very soon, we will be publishing books by top celebrity authors and fending off calls from *Loose Women* and *The Paul O'Grady Show*.

Lovely Richard eyes our skinny lattes greedily. 'They look good,' he says. 'I'd die for a coffee.' He flashes his big brown eyes at me.

'I can take a hint,' I say. 'What do you want?'

'Cappuccino. Lots of chocolate on top.' He hands over some money. 'A brownie or two maybe?'

I shrug on my coat. 'If Antonio Banderas phones for me tell him I won't be long.'

Outside, the hit of cold air takes my breath away. I had to scrape inch-thick ice off my car this morning, surely the first sign of the onset of winter. I wonder if we will have a white Christmas this year.

Plodding through the car park to Coffee Café, I pass by my car and glance over towards it. Something has been stuck behind one of its windscreen wipers and, eager to stretch my time out of the office on management business, I wander over to have a look.

It's a hand-written poem on posh paper. The writing is round and tidy. The writing of someone who has taken a lot of trouble. I ease it out and read it.

'*Some noses are red,*
some noses are blue,
I'm looking forward to Christmas,
Are you?'

I feel my forehead crease in a frown. Possibly not the most romantic verse I could think of, but I wonder who put it there. I look back towards the office. Mmm.

There's no queue in Coffee Café, for once. The guy behind the counter waves when he sees me.

'Hi,' he says as he loads up a tray with blueberry muffins.

'Hi.'

He's wearing a fur fabric Santa hat that is playing Christmassy tunes, jingling away as he works. That must be deeply irritating.

Currently playing is that cheery old favourite by Mud – 'Lonely This Christmas'. How true, I mutter to myself through gritted teeth. How bloody true.

'How's the glamorous world of publishing today?' the guy asks as I order Lovely Richard's coffee.

'Wonderful.' Little does he know that I'm currently editing a book about how to build an authentic American Indian tepee using only recycled materials. It's not exactly *Sex and The City*, is it? 'How's business here?'

'Booming,' he tells me with a smile. His eyes crinkle very nicely when he grins. 'Thanks to all the dedicated coffee addicts around here.'

I can hold my hand up to that. As I wait for Lovely Richard's coffee, I pick out two scrummy-looking brownies and wonder if he'd miss a tiny bite from one of the corners.

While I'm here I might as well get a few bits for Chrissie and myself. I pick out some chocolate-coated flapjack. And maybe we could do with some more coffees too. Our days go so much quicker when we recklessly eat and drink our way through them. What the hell. I ask the guy in the jingly hat for two more cappuccinos.

'Thanks,' I say when my order comes.

'My pleasure,' the guy says and, having come for one cup, I struggle out with a tray of cups and several paper bags stuffed with goodies.

Back at the office, I hand over Lovely Richard's coffee, brownies and his change. He thanks me profusely and wanders off. I tell Chrissie about the note under my windscreen wiper.

'Ooo,' she says. 'I bet Lovely Richard put it there.'

'Don't be silly.'

'Who else would it be?' she wants to know. 'I'll hate you if he fancies you and not me. I'll stop being your best friend.'

The next day when I'm dispatched for our morning sustenance order, I notice that a single red rose has been slipped under my windscreen wiper. There's a gift tag attached to it with a neat note – same handwriting as the poem. Perhaps I should consider a career as an ace detective.

Twenty-four days to Christmas, it says. *I can't wait.*

And, don't you dare laugh, I think I'm slightly more sprightly in step than I usually am when I continue across the car park to Coffee Café.

Inside, the man with the jingly hat is exuding Slade's 'Merry Christmas Everybody' and he's mad busy.

He nods briefly at my rose as he hands over my order. 'Nice.'

'Yeah. It was on my windscreen.'

'Romantic.'

'Depends who put it there,' I say in what I think is an enigmatic manner.

Back in the office, I take the rose and put it in a prominent place in a left-over, rinsed-out polystyrene Coffee Café cup on my desk.

When Lovely Richard comes to put in his afternoon order, Chrissie and I wait for his reaction. A faint flushing, a sudden coyness. Nothing. Nada. He doesn't even notice it.

'It's just a ploy,' Chrissie tells me sagely. 'It's him all right. I know men.'

I don't point out that she hasn't known a man for a long time. Me neither.

And so it continues throughout December. Every day something new and wonderful is sneaked under one of my car's windscreen wipers. Every day Chrissie and I fail to see who the culprit is, despite spending an inordinate amount of time staring out of the window when we should, in fact, be working.

So far I've received – in no particular order – a stuffed snowman, star-shaped chocolates, Christmas socks, flashing Santa earrings, fluffy reindeer antlers, a CD of Christmas songs old and new. And other festive goodies too many and varied to mention, all of them with a cryptic note attached. It's like having my own brilliant, car-based Advent calendar. I'm feeling so unusually in the festive swing, that the CD of Christmas songs blasts out of my car every morning on my way to work. Even Shakin' Stevens and 'Merry Christmas Everyone' can't put me in a bad mood.

Chrissie, however, is becoming very morose whenever Lovely Richard calls by our desk. She is convinced that any day now he will be proposing marriage to me at the very least. But, despite the flowing range of thoughtful little presents, he still hasn't made any further approach towards me – other than hanging round our desk more and more when *he*, in fact, should be working. There's been no intimate little comments, no trying to catch up with me by the lift or the water cooler, no hints that he might have the hots for me. Nothing.

Pondering this deeply, I take the office coffee order and plod out, weaving through the cars in the car park, to see my friend at Coffee Café. I hang back until he's served everyone else and there's just the two of us in the shop.

'Aren't you getting tired of that relentlessly cheerful hat yet?'

'No. Are you?'

Surprisingly not. I shrug. Today's offering is Kylie Minogue and 'Santa Baby.' I'm sure I will do soon.

'Signed any A list celebrity authors yet?' my Coffee Café friend wants to know as he fiddles about making two frothy cappuccinos.

'Yes. Jordan and David Beckham. That was this morning.' I select some particularly delectable pieces of caramel shortbread. 'Put in a bid for Starbucks yet?'

'Yes,' he says and treats me to an evil cackle. 'My quest for world domination has begun. I want to open a chain that spreads across Britain, then America and the rest of the known world.'

'Lovely.' He'll probably be able to retire in a few years from what we at Earth Publishing alone spend in here. 'I like a man with ambition.'

He raises his eyebrows. 'See you this afternoon. I have some snowmen gingerbread biscuits coming in. I'll save some for you.'

'Do you like Christmas?' I ask with a frown.

'Love it,' he says with a smile. 'It's the time for giving.'

So. Now it's the eighteenth of December and our office party is in a scant two days' time. Chrissie and I are still dateless. I am still receiving gorgeous little gifts on a daily basis. Gifts that warm my heart. Someone out there loves me. I just wish I knew who it was.

Everyone else brings along their partners to the party and we'll look like such sad sacks if we have to sit next to each other – again. Lovely Richard still hasn't made a move and, if he's going to, I do wish he'd get on with it. The extent of his lurking around our desk is reaching embarrassing proportions. He is in danger of being classed as a stalker.

'What are we going to do?' Chrissie wails. 'We should rent escorts for the night. Ones that look as if they're in boy bands.'

'We can't do that. Be sensible,' I tut. 'There is no shame in going to the office party alone.'

'There is,' she moans.

'It's no good. I can take this no longer.' I stand up from my desk. 'Time for some calorific comfort,' I announce.

'You always go for the coffee these days,' Chrissie says. 'Don't you want me to take a turn? You used to always complain that I didn't do it often enough.'

'I don't mind,' I insist. And for some reason I flush. Even though I'm depressed about the impending office party, I take the stairs with a spring in my step.

The guy from Coffee Café is catering for our Christmas Eve lunch at work and, when I reach the car park, I remember that I should have brought the list of sandwiches and goodies that we want, to discuss with him. He's building up a great business over there and I'm really pleased for him. I turn and dash back to my desk to collect it.

When I get there, Chrissie is sitting in a catatonic state. Her face is as white as the driven snow – apart from two bright pink circles on her cheeks.

'What?' I say. 'What's happened?'

'You'll never guess.'

'You've been sacked.'

'No. No.'

'*I've* been sacked.'

Chrissie looks up at me. Her eyes are glazed and staring. 'Lovely Richard has asked me to be his date for the office party.'

'No.' I sink to my seat.

'It wasn't you he fancied after all,' she says and I look for a hint of smugness, but there isn't one. 'It was me.'

I go round to her side of the desk and give her a big hug. 'I'm so pleased for you.'

'So am I,' she says. 'But what will you do? And, if it isn't Lovely Richard, who's putting all those pressies on your car?'

I only wish I knew. To divert my brain, I pick up the Christmas list for Coffee Café and head out there. As I make my way through the car park, a few flakes of snow start to fall. Looks like it might be a white Christmas after all. Nice.

The doorbell dings my arrival and I shake the snow from my hair, making a mess on his floor.

'Very festive,' my friend behind the counter says.

'I brought the Christmas food list for you,' I tell him. 'Nothing too complicated. We all eat it and then scarper as early as we can get away with.'

'Sounds like a good idea.'

'Most people have got places to go, I guess. People to see . . .' my voice trails away.

'Have you got any plans for Christmas this year?' he asks.

'Me?' I shake my head again. No snow storm on the floor this time. 'No,' I admit. 'Nothing.' I try to make light of my predicament. 'All quiet on the Western front. You know how it is.'

'Yes,' he agrees. 'I do.'

And then because he's studying me rather intently, I hastily turn my attention to my list. 'Here's the list.'

I hand it over. It's suddenly hot in here. Must be because I've rushed in from the cold.

'I wrote out a quick quote for you,' he says. 'Sorry. I didn't have time to put it on the computer.'

He gives me the piece of paper, headed with the Coffee Café logo. My mouth drops open, but it's nothing to do with the

114

price noted down. I stare back at him. I'd know that hand-writing anywhere. I've seen it often enough over the last few weeks.

'It's . . . it's . . . you!' I manage to stammer.

'Perhaps it's time we were formally introduced,' he says. 'I'm Josh. I hope you've liked your gifts.'

'Maria,' I reply. 'I've loved them all. That was such a kind thing of you to do.'

Josh shrugs. 'I do have an ulterior motive.'

I wait with bated breath.

'I have no one to spend Christmas with this year. I thought you might like to share it with me.'

'I'd love to,' I breathe.

Mariah Carey starts up on Josh's fur hat. The sounds of 'All I Want For Christmas is You,' fills Coffee Café with festive cheer.

'How appropriate,' my friend observes.

Then Josh comes round the counter, takes my hands in his and we dance together as we sing along.

The Love of Christmas Past

I gaze at the Christmas tree lights, sparkling, white, and my eyes fill with tears. The clock strikes midnight, announcing that we've slipped into Christmas Day. The room is suddenly chilly and I bend to stoke the few embers in the grate, hoping to elicit some meagre warmth.

When I turn again, Joe's standing in the room, over by the French windows.

'Hello, Joe.'

'Marcie.' He comes towards me. 'How are you? You're looking great.'

'I'm fine.' I know that I'm not looking great. I'm looking tired and I feel old. This year has been a difficult one and it's taken its toll.

Joe takes in the room. The heavy velvet curtains are drawn against the cold, except on the French doors. Through the panes, I can see the moon bathe the frosty garden, giving the plants and path a silver sheen. I take greater care with this room than the others. I like it to look nice, welcoming. There are candles, rich and sturdy, scented with cinnamon, orange, pomegranate. The fireplace is adorned with Christmas cards – some of them from old friends that Joe and I had together.

'Christmas again,' he says. 'Already. It comes round so quickly.'

If you ask me, I don't think it comes round quickly enough. I would like it to be Christmas, every week, every day.

He tries to look cheerful. 'The tree's looking wonderful.'

A blue spruce this year, so tall that we had to take off some of the top to get it into the room. 'Thank you.'

We're formal with each other and it's hard that we have to waste these precious stolen moments on pleasantries. But how else are we to be with each other after so long? I can hardly rush into his arms.

His face looks paler than usual, anguished and I would give anything, *anything*, to be able to hold him. 'Are you all right?'

Joe shrugs. 'Oh, you know.'

And I do. Yet we're awkward with each other and that's the bit I hate the most.

He drifts a little closer, attempting to bridge the gap between us. 'I tried to stay,' he says. 'You know that.'

'I do.'

'I fought so very hard.'

'I know that, my love.' Joe's a fighter. That's what everyone said.

'I hated leaving. But I simply couldn't stay.'

I nod, unable to speak. A cold tear rolls down my cheek.

'What are you doing for Christmas?'

I manage a weak smile. 'My son's coming home.'

Joe looks surprised. 'You have a son?'

'Yes. Jonathan. We call him Jonty. He's nineteen now.'

'Almost a man.' He frowns. 'You've told me this before?'

'Yes. You'd like him. He's clever, articulate. Very funny.' He looks just like his father too.

'You must be very proud of him.'

'I am.'

'Perhaps I could meet him one day,' Joe suggests. 'I'd like that.'

'I'm not sure.' I can't face his dark, searching eyes. 'It might not be possible.'

'Oh. Right.' Joe wrings his hands. 'This is a terrible situation.'

'Yes.'

'I love you,' he says, bleakly. 'I always will.'

'And I love you.' More than life itself. I go to touch his face and then check myself. It's too hard. So very hard.

There's a noise overhead, a squeak of floorboards and a flutter starts in my chest. It will be over, too soon, this treasured time. Don't come down, I think. Don't come down. Not yet. But, sure enough, a moment later there's the sound of a heavy footstep on the stairs.

'That's my husband.'

He looks startled. 'You're married?'

'You know this, Joe.'

He hangs his head and says, 'You could have waited.'

'I did, my love. I waited five long years.' I was a single mum, alone and lonely with a small boy to care for. What else was I to do?

'Oh.'

'You have to go now, Joe.'

'Yes.' He looks at me bleakly. 'I love you so much.'

'I love you too. For ever.'

'For all eternity.'

The door opens and Oliver stands there in his dressing gown, hair tousled, eyes heavy with sleep.

'I thought I heard voices,' he says.

I look to where Joe was standing but, already, he's faded away.

'No. Just talking to myself.'

Oliver comes to hold me and his body is warm, comforting. 'I know this is a difficult time of year for you, but Jonty will be home later. That will cheer you up.'

'Yes.'

He rubs my arms. 'You're freezing cold. It's draughty in here. Are the windows closed properly?'

'I'll check.'

'Come to bed.'

'You go up. I've got a few more things to do, then I'll be with you.'

Oliver lets go of me. 'Don't be long, sweetheart. You don't want to be tired on Christmas Day.'

I smile, more wearily than I'd like, and let my hand linger in his. 'A moment longer, that's all.'

He leaves and I stand still, listening to him climb the stairs again. He's a good man. Solid, dependable and I love him. But he's not Joe.

I go to the French windows and look out. I think I catch a glimpse of Joe in his favourite place in the garden. But, of course, I'm mistaken. I won't see him again until next Christmas.

'Merry Christmas, my love,' I murmur.

And I think I hear Joe whisper it back to me.

Cold Turkey

I can't stand turkey. Okay, so it's a reasonably-priced white meat, versatile, low in fat and, supposedly, good for the heart. I have no quibble with that. Particularly. It's just all the other crap that goes with it. The cranberry sauce, the Brussels sprouts, the chipolata sausages wrapped in streaky bacon, the cheap crackers, the gaudy party hats, the waiting by the phone alone on Christmas Day in the vain hope that your married lover might be able to sneak away from the bosom of his family for a rushed two-second call. That's what I really can't stand.

I'm thirty years old, intelligent (questionable given current situation), financially solvent (also questionable after pre-Christmas spending frenzy) and gainfully employed as a human resources manager for a multi-national corporation. It's just my own resources I have trouble managing.

I have hair that wouldn't look out of place being swished around in a L'Oreal advert, porcelain skin and cheekbones to die for. So why am I staring at a pale, miserable face in a holly-festooned mirror, that looks back at me mournfully like the Ghost of Christmas Past? Because, on the down side, I have legs like a rugby player, a propensity to chain eat Toffee Crisps in stressful situations and it's already twelve o'clock and the aforementioned married lover hasn't troubled British Telecom with his custom once.

It was the same last year – that's the stupid thing. And the year before. I could go to my parents. My sister's there this year, having left her husband for the man at the Bradford and Bingley building society, who decided after three weeks that he couldn't live without his children and returned, suitably penitent, to the marital bed. There's a lot of it about.

We all get on well, my family. We don't usually try to kill each other over the Queen's speech, we all like to watch the much-repeated Christmas edition of *Only Fools and Horses* – even though we all know the script off by heart now – and we all marvel at the fact that my mother sticks religiously to the hideous, time-honoured tradition of cooking a ham just for Boxing Day even though none of us ever eats it. So there is no need for me to be this sad old bat with swollen, red eyes and tear-stained cheeks, looking fretfully at the turkey sitting patiently in the roasting pan, which, even though it was the smallest bird that Waitrose could offer, still looks like something that has wandered out of *Jurassic Park*.

I have a pile of peeled potatoes languishing in a pan of salted water. Carrots. Parsnips. The ubiquitous Brussels sprouts. You name it, I've got it. Christmas pudding, brandy sauce (carton of), assorted nuts (and I don't even *like* nuts that much), Eat Me dates, Turkish Delight and all the other unnecessary little indulgences essential to make Christmas tick. You see, this year he said that he would come to me. He would try *very hard* to come to me. He would find a reason to nip out at an opportune moment, skipping the traditional family lunch that is being shared with in-laws, out-laws, wife, kids, cats, dogs and, no doubt, the festive hamster that his youngest son has brought home from school for the holidays. Feigning some disaster that had befallen his accountancy firm, (Fire? Flood? Famine?) he would rush from his home to my waiting arms and eat Waitrose turkey breast with me. And do you know what the really sad thing is? Even sadder than the raw meat, the uncooked potatoes and the ton of prepared Brussels? The sad thing is, I believed him.

The weather is bleak. Not a white Christmas – a grey, anonymous day marks the birth of the most enduring idol in history and the start of another round of family rows that will take until Easter to sort out. The sky is the colour of a school skirt and it looks seriously cold outside. I need fresh air, though, however bracing. Besides, how much longer can I sit by my flame-effect gas fire and pretend that I don't care that the phone is staring silently and knowingly at the back of my head?

My coat is warm and offers the comfort of weight that the arms of a lover should be providing. I walk my usual route towards Battersea Park and the tall, solid columns of the defunct power station look down at me questioningly and say, *What on earth are you doing alone on Christmas Day?* With a hollow little shock inside, I acknowledge that I feel as powerless as they now are, and if I gave them an answer, I realise it would sound pathetic. I grip my bag of stale bread too tightly, my mind going over old ground as surely as my feet are. I am bright. I am bubbly. I am a very popular woman. (Have I told you this before? Hard lines. My mother tells me often enough.) So why am I putting myself through this torture? I love him. Is it so difficult to understand?

The seething mass of humanity that gives this ragged piece of ground its buzz and colour is conspicuous by its absence. I know where they are. They're all at home snuggled in with their loved ones, stuffing their faces with turkey. I can hear my lonely steps echoing on the crumbling concrete pavements and I pretend that I don't care. The boating lake is half-frozen, littered with crisp packets and empty Tango cans and the ducks sit on the ice looking cheesed off. I rustle my bag of stale bread at them encouragingly and they stare at me with disdain. Perhaps they hate stale bread as much as I hate turkey.

There is a man at the other side of the lake, next to the boats abandoned bottom-up for the winter. He, too, is clutching a paper bag and is making duck-like noises, which convince me, but clearly not the ducks. I walk closer to where he is standing, which surprises me because I'm normally a complete wimp when it comes to strangers.

'Quack, quack,' he shouts enthusiastically at his reluctant dinner guests.

He looks up at me and smiles. It's slightly crooked, but open and friendly. I smile back, a little shyly perhaps.

'Hi,' he says.

'Hi.'

He dips into the bag and pulls out his offering.

'*Pain au chocolat?*'

I am impressed.

'Fresh, too,' he offers. 'Supposed to be this morning's breakfast.' He rips one into small pieces and throws it onto the water, temptingly close to the ducks.

'You weren't hungry?'

'No,' he says sadly. 'I wasn't.'

The ducks scramble to their feet and waddle across the ice, their feet slipping on the smooth surface which robs them of their natural grace. I guess we all lose our footing when the ground is unfamiliar. Like ducks out of water.

'I wonder if their bottoms get cold,' he queries, 'sitting on the ice like that?'

I shrug. 'I expect so.'

'They look about as miserable as you,' he says kindly.

I laugh, and a little happy bubble pushes inside my pain. I look at the stranger. He's tall with brown hair flecked with auburn that would catch the sun if there was any. His eyes are greeny-brown and they match his coat, which is long and a bit *Doctor Who*-ish. He has the look of a hungover leprechaun, slightly cheeky with red-rimmed eyes beneath eyebrows that are permanently raised as if in surprise. He would look better if he wore sunglasses.

'You don't look so great yourself,' I tell him.

He smirks. 'I guess not.'

I open my bag and frown into it. 'I don't think they'll eat this now you've indulged them with French delights.'

He takes a couple of step towards me and I see that he has been crying. 'What've you got?'

'Stale Hovis.'

'Staple diet of a duck,' he assures me.

'Staple diet of a human resources manager too,' I assure him.

'We could give them the bread and eat the *pain au chocolat* ourselves,' he suggests. 'We wouldn't want them growing up spoiled and not appreciating the value of money.'

We throw the bread to them together, tearing it into shreds to make it easily digestible. His hands are warm and soft when they accidentally brush against mine and they make me shiver inside. Retiring to the terrace of the shuttered café, we sit on the few plastic chairs that remain at the mercy of the elements, eating the greasy, calorie-laden chocolaty bread in silence. When we are finished and have licked our fingers, he holds out his hand.

'Danny Kerrick,' he says as I take it and note that it is faintly sticky with sugar.

'Tara Lewis,' I say, returning the compliment.

He turns his body further towards me, but gazes out across the lake.

'So, Tara Lewis, why are you feeding the ducks alone on Christmas Day?' he asks.

'Because,' I pause, swallowing the lump that has come to my throat, 'I have a married lover,' I answer. 'Who promised me he would come, but hasn't.'

The corners of his mouth turn down in sympathy. 'That's terrible,' he says, his soft Irish burr deepening slightly.

'Why are you doing the same thing, Danny Kerrick?'

He looks back at me. 'Because I had a married lover too. Until yesterday.' There is a smile on his lips that doesn't match the sadness in his eyes. 'I didn't quite get the Christmas present I expected.'

'I'm sorry,' I say.

He studies his feet. 'I'm not sure if I am.' Suddenly, his smile warms and he glances up. 'I expect you've a cupboard full of nuts and dates and Turkish Delight. Little things to make your lover's heart glad?'

'Yes,' I giggle, feeling embarrassed.

'So have I,' he admits.

'The *pain au chocolat* were for her?'

He shakes his head. 'I doubted it even as I bought them.'

We watch the ducks settle back on the ice, fluffing up their feathers and lowering themselves gingerly. They might be cold and miserable, but at least they're not turkeys.

'I have pans full of peeled veg and,' I nod at our feather friends, 'a distant cousin in a roasting tin.'

'What will you do with it now?'

I grimace, thinking of how much it had all cost, how long it had taken me to shop, how silly I feel now. 'Bin it,' I say with venom. 'I hate turkey, anyway.'

'It seems a waste.'

'I couldn't eat it. Unless . . .' I laugh at my own stupidity. 'No.' It's the sort of thing people say in afternoon soap operas, the heroine going girly and coquettish and here I am doing it too.

'What?' Danny is frowning.

'Well, unless . . .' I will stay here stammering for ever, if I don't blurt it out. 'Would you like to come back to my place and we'll eat together?'

125

The permanently surprised eyebrows rise even further.

'Unless, of course, you've made other plans. You will have done, of course. It was silly of me to ask . . .'

'I've no plans,' he says in a rush. Then he breaks into a casual smile. 'Except that Julia Roberts said she might pop round, but I'm sure she wouldn't mind finding me out.'

'Not this once,' I agree.

We stand and shake the untidy flakes of *pain au chocolat* from our coats.

'It's not far,' I say.

'Shall we take a lap of the pond?' he asks. 'Then we can pretend we came here for a purpose.'

'I did come here with a purpose,' I protest.

'What?'

'Running away from my misery.'

'That's not a purpose,' he informs me with a grin. 'That's a reaction.'

'It feels good to be outside,' I say.

'With someone to talk to.'

'Yes.' I smile and watch my own breath hang on the air. 'It's as if the cobwebs are being blown from my fuzzy brain.'

He walks closer to me as we complete our stroll round the dirty, desolate pond and it doesn't faze me at all. It's nice. He feels sort of safe and there's no need to watch over our shoulders in case people we know might spy us in places where we shouldn't be.

'The turkey awaits,' I say and we set off home.

The heat in the flat is oppressive after the sharp day outside. The sort of heat that steams up your glasses when you come inside – if you wear them. Danny doesn't wear glasses, but he unwinds his scarf and abandons his coat with an alacrity that says he is steaming up inside. I throw open the windows, letting the cold air refresh the room so that I won't become fugged again and take our coats out into the hall.

126

When I come back, Danny is walking round the room, casually examining the contents of my life, and I'm surprised that I don't resent the intrusion. He stops at the bookcase. 'James Joyce,' he says, looking impressed.

'It's not mine,' I explain, feeling self-conscious. 'I read the Dan Browns on the tube.' I indicate my pile of well-thumbed paperbacks that have been pushed to one side of the top shelf to make room for my lover's preferred choice of literature.

He wanders to the CD player and flicks through the discs. 'I guess you're the Simply Red and not the Bach.'

'You guess right.' I couldn't help but smile. 'And the George Michael.'

He picks up the photograph next to the phone. 'Is this the absent lover?'

'Edward,' I confirm.

'Half-man, half-real-life Hollywood hero,' he says, his mouth tightening in what might be disapproval.

I flush. It was a photograph of Edward on holiday in the Caribbean and he has a deep mahogany hue and looks much older than me. Which he is. Danny is right, it has a vaguely unreal quality to it, sort of Kilroy Silk meets *Thunderbirds* or an advertisement for a male hair dye that says *Hate that grey? Wash it away*! It used to be my favourite photograph of him. We've never had one taken together. This is all I have.

'He's very sophisticated,' I say, feeling anything but.

'He looks great,' Danny replies, sounding unconvinced. 'I'm sure he adores you.'

Our eyes meet and we acknowledge the fact that if he did adore me, Edward would be here right now. I look away and as I do a slight jolt goes through me. The little red light on the answer-phone is winking seductively at me.

'I have a message,' I say and make a mental note that my heart is playing 'do-wah diddy-diddy dum diddy-do'.

'Shall I make myself scarce?'

'No, no,' I insist, with a careless wave of my hand. 'We're not the billing and cooing type,' I reply, wondering for the first time why we aren't. 'There's some red wine open in the kitchen and the glasses are in the cupboard above it. Why don't you pour us a glass?'

My fingers hesitate as I switch the machine to play. What if Edward has called to say he's on his way round? What will he think if he finds Danny here? It would be unfair of me to ask him to leave now. The machine clicks and whirs into life and eventually throws my mother's voice out into the room.

'I hope you're out having fun,' she says in a warning tone. 'Don't be alone. Come over. Your sister's here. We've got plenty of turkey. It's your mother,' she adds, in case I was ever in any doubt.

Danny has already switched on the cooker and is mixing Paxo in a bowl by the time I join him in the kitchen. It's clear from the expression on his face that he can tell I've been crying. Only a few measly snivelled tears, but crying nevertheless. His look of complete understanding and sympathy turns on the tap in my heart again.

'Here,' he hands me a glass, holding my fingers over the stem, his own gentle pressure urging me not to clench too tight and shatter it. The wine is luxurious, deep red. Rich, dark, the colour of love. Penfold Bin 28 shiraz. Edward's favourite. 'Chin up,' Danny says, tilting my face and running his thumb gently across my skin.

My chin falls and I cry some more. Danny pulls me to him and wraps his arms round me. They're strong and supportive even though he is still a stranger to me. Someone I have just met in the park. His jumper is soft against my cheek and smells of cinnamon and stale smoke and ink jet printers.

'I've been there,' he says softly. 'I know what you're going through.'

I think his *pain au chocolat* woman must be mad to have left him, but it doesn't seem appropriate to voice it. I wipe my eyes on the kitchen roll he hands me and sniff attractively as I push away from him. 'Let's give this bird some grief,' I say with conviction.

Danny leans back on the cupboards, crossing one long leg over the other. He puts down his wine glass decisively. The leprechaun's eyes twinkle in my strategically angled spotlights and they gaze directly at me. He bites his lip nervously. 'I have a confession to make.'

'Do I really want to hear this?' I ask cautiously. I have learned to my cost that honesty is not always the best policy.

'I think it's wise.'

He twists his hands together. 'Before we go any further.'

'Okay,' I say nonchalantly and notice that my stomach has clenched.

'I'm vegetarian,' he says.

We stare at each other open-mouthed.

'I am too,' I confess.

We both smirk like naughty schoolchildren caught stealing Jammie Dodgers, until I start to laugh, at first tentatively and then uncontrollably, and it is such a long-forgotten act, this unfettered hilarity, that it makes my cheeks ache with pure pleasure. Danny joins in, guffawing maniacally, clutching his sides as I do, until the tears stream down our cheeks. Then we cry the laughter away with the serious tears of the emotionally drained, and I cross the kitchen so that he can hold me some more. We stand entwined until the heaving, racking sobs leave our bodies and we are spent and sensible once again.

'What a pair,' he says lightly, to cover our embarrassment.

'Are you hungry?' I say, relying on the British propensity to substitute food for difficult scenes.

'Starving,' he replies.

129

Danny says he is sure he has seen Ken Hom do something exciting with Brussels sprouts, so we chop the languishing vegetables into tiny pieces and stir-fry them, flinging in a jar of yellow bean sauce that was lurking at the back of the cupboard for good measure. I throw in a handful of the cashews (also Edward's favourites) with a flourish and a bitter little smile. There is some fried rice in a margarine carton in the freezer and I defrost it in the microwave. The abandoned turkey eyes us dolefully.

We observe some festive formalities by eating at the table, cosily set for two. I light the romantic fragrant candle as an act of pique and we crack our Christmas crackers, groan at the feeble jokes and admire each other's purple paper hats which are, obviously, far too big. The relaxed atmosphere only falters slightly as we toast absent friends with the remains of Edward's Shiraz.

The Christmas pudding and brandy sauce sit heavily on top of our stir-fry, but we plough our way stoically through it and even squeeze in a Mr Kipling's mince pie on top out of politeness. We nurse cups of freshly ground coffee from the cafetière which wears a Santa's suit to keep it warm and talk of our lives. An hour has gone by before I know it and, as I glance at the clock, I realise I haven't thought of Edward once.

The afternoon melts into the evening and I turn on the lamps to ward off the darkness and light some more candles, giving the room a mellow glow and the scent of *Joyeux Noel* (whatever that is). Danny insists on washing up and takes his duties seriously, donning bright pink marigolds and a reindeer apron before starting. I lie on the sofa, swirling a hefty measure of brandy in a glass, shoes abandoned, wiggling my toes in my tights and massaging my stomach which strains in an un-comely fashion against its Lycra bondage. The knot of tension which has been a permanent and unwanted feature throughout my relationship with Edward has gone and, though it may well just have been squished out of the way by sheer weight of food, I feel it is not in small part due to Danny's company. He whistles tunelessly as he washes up, clanking the dishes together with cheerful abandon. I want him to be finished soon, to come and sit with me, to tell me some more of his silly wandering stories, heavily laced with Irish blarney.

My wish comes true after five minutes' wait. He flops down beside me on the sofa, brushing his hair back from his face, plumping the cushions and putting my feet up on to his lap with the comfortable ease of a life-long friend.

'Happy?' he says.

And the strange thing is, I say yes.

We listen to 'The Christmas Album' (Bing Crosby, Judy Garland, Ella Fitzgerald) a selection of songs destined to make you wish Christmas was how it used to be and not the commercial, fraught mess it is now. Bought, of course, with Edward in mind. Although it's pleasantly soothing, it is his type of music not mine and I consider how little we really have in common. The most obvious being that only one of us is free. Free? Am I really free, tied into this triangle that stretches eternally before me?

Danny's head lies back against the sofa, his eyes closed, humming to the music, a pink alcohol-induced flush to his cheeks. My insides glow and I smile at him without meaning to. As if sensing my mood, his hand reaches out and massages my ankles. It isn't a sexual touch, just comforting, but it sends a thrill through my body nevertheless.

The telephone shrills just as Bing tells us he's dreaming of a white Christmas just like the ones he used to know, and makes us both jump. Danny's eyes shoot open and we both sit bolt upright as I rearrange my skirt feeling ridiculously guilty. By the time I have mustered my scattered thoughts, the answerphone has cut in.

131

'It's Edward,' a croaking voice says in hushed tones.

A needless introduction, just like my mother's (what a terrifying thought) and I can picture his hand cupping the mouthpiece, his eyes darting fearfully over his shoulder. I perch on the edge of the sofa and listen, for some reason reluctant to speak to the love of my life.

'Look,' he continues, whispering earnestly. 'I can't talk for long. It's going to be impossible to get away.'

Why does this not surprise me?

'I've got a terrible cold, Luke's gone down with tonsillitis, the mother-in-law's pissed and the fucking hamster's escaped and chewed through the Christmas tree lights.'

Danny laughs at that and I grin back.

'I'm sorry,' Edward says flatly. 'But you know how it is.'

I know only too well. I walk to the wall and pull the telephone plug out of its socket a touch too fiercely, cutting Edward off in his prime. I wonder if he would have remembered to wish me a happy Christmas.

Danny stands up, uncomfortable now. He puts his half-drunk brandy on the coffee table, careful not to clink the glass. 'Look,' he says, shifting from foot to foot, 'this must be difficult for you.' He shrugs uneasily. 'If you want to be alone, I'll leave. I've enjoyed it. It's been the best Christmas Day I've had for a long time. You've been very kind.'

'I think I've been very selfish,' I say. 'Keeping you here, when you probably had a million other things to do.'

'I can wash my hair any old day of the week.' He flicks his fringe back for effect and makes me laugh again.

'You're very silly.'

His eyes look troubled. 'I don't want to overstep the mark.'

'What mark?' I tease.

'*The* mark,' he says, the twinkle returning.

'I want you to stay.' I'm astonished at how brazen I sound

when I'm attempting to be sincere. 'You can help me to finish the leftovers.'

'Cold turkey?' he asks.

I nod in what I believe is a hopeful fashion. Cold turkey. 'Something like that,' I answer.

'Cold turkey can sometimes be the best thing,' Danny advises.

'Even for vegetarians?'

As Danny pulls me to him I notice the mistletoe stuck with Blu-Tac above the kitchen door. 'Even for vegetarians,' he says.

On the CD player Judy Garland urges us to have ourselves a merry little Christmas. Somehow I think we might.

If you enjoyed this exclusive short story collection from Carole Matthews, then read on for an extract from the *Sunday Times* Top Five bestselling

Paper Hearts and Summer Kisses

A heart-warming and poignant novel of romance, family and second chances, *Paper Hearts and Summer Kisses* is Carole Matthews at her outstanding best.

Available now!

Chapter One

'No. No. No.' Much groaning. It's five o'clock in the morning and my wake-up alarm is ringing its head off. My dear son, Finn, has set it to play an altogether too cheerful 'How D'Ya Like Your Eggs in the Morning?'. Right now, I'd opt for served on a silver salver by a butler at an infinitely more civilised hour of the day. This getting up at the crack of dawn every day is too cruel. I put out a hand and fumble to turn it off, knocking my phone to the floor and out of reach. Which is just as well as the temptation to smash it is overwhelming. I flop back and pull my pillow over my head. I hate five o'clock in the morning. Hate it. With a passion. Yet it comes round far too quickly every day.

I'd really love to stay here and have a much-needed duvet day, but I catch my commuter coach into London in less than an hour and any thought of dilly-dallying in bed is out of the question. Though I might be a reluctant getter-upper, I'm actually quite a loyal employee. To my eternal credit, I've rarely had a day off sick in the eighteen years I've worked for the same company. Impressive, eh? Well, I think so.

Another reason I can't delay any longer is that Dean Martin

is still crooning into the carpet and the dog is starting to whine along too. The only way I can shut them both up is to get out of bed. I am resigning myself to my fate, but I still do it with much groaning.

'Come on, Christie Chapman,' I mutter to no one but myself. 'Let's be having you.'

I move my bedfellows as kindly as I can – two cats and the aforementioned dog. Eric wags his tail, does a full circle of the bed and settles down again. How I envy him. The cats – Lily and Pixel – reluctantly rouse themselves from sleep and both eye me with a depth of loathing that only our feline friends can convey. It's the same every day. They hate the alarm too but, like me, you think they'd be used to it by now.

Quietening the chirpy Dean en route, I stagger towards the bathroom. If they ever need any extras on *The Walking Dead*, I could do it. Without the need for a costume. Or make-up.

I didn't really get enough sleep last night as I went to bed way too late. I wasn't out partying or anything. I don't want to give you the impression that I actually have a life. Oh no. Sad single that I am, I spend my sad single evenings paper crafting while watching rubbish on telly. To pass the hours, I make cards, gift tags, scrapbooks, that kind of thing. I'm currently in the throes of making a birthday card for a friend. My lovely mate, Sarah Plimmer, is about to turn forty and she's really special to me, so I want to do something totally fab for her. The perfect design is eluding me. Consequently, I spent aeons on Pinterest – as you do – and fell into bed at midnight when I really like to be tucked up at half past ten. Latest.

The sight of my morning self in the mirror is truly scary. My forty-odd-year-old face takes quite a lot of time to reassemble itself into the right symmetry after being reshaped by the pillow all night. Seriously, it's a good half-hour these days before the creases go. I keep thinking I should get some decent eye cream to slather onto the puffy bags that greet me pre-dawn, but I never quite manage that level of beauty routine. I'm a sort of soap and water kinda gal. But I'm getting to the age where I need considerably more help than that.

In my sleepy state, I get on the scales. That always scares me as well. I don't know why I do it. I like to think that a daily weigh-in will help me to keep my middle-aged spread in check. In reality, it just depresses me and has me reaching for a comforting chocolate bar instead. If I had any sense, I should just throw them in the bin.

I rely on the power of hot water to bring me back to life and prepare me for the long day ahead. I put on my frog shower cap. I bought it because it's green and yellow and has those big white eyes where the black bits rotate. I thought it would cheer me up at the start of my day. It doesn't.

I'm hoping that I can get away without washing my hair for another day. It's long and brown – as my plug hole can attest to – and I keep meaning to get it cut short so that it will be more manageable, but never quite find the time. I'd like one of those styles that you wash and go in three minutes, even though I think they might be an urban myth. There are a few grey hairs showing too, but I'm trying to put off dyeing as it will not only require even more time, but also additional expense that I can well do without. Currently, I'm just pulling them out as I see them and hoping that they don't start coming through so thick and fast that I go bald.

I keep my eyes closed in the shower so that I can hold onto the pretence of sleep for just a little while longer. I don't mind commuting. Actually, yes I do. It's four precious hours out of my day that I could, surely, utilise in a much better way. It's mind-numbing, expensive and exhausting. On the plus side, I avoid the hideous crush of the train and travel by comfortable coach which picks me up at the end of my road and deposits me right outside my office on the Embankment. There is a train station in Wolverton, where I live, but it's at the other end of the town and the journey would cost twice as much *plus* involve a long walk, a train and a tube. Hideous. On the coach I sit still for two hours each way and they serve me coffee. I think that last bit was the deal clincher.

I'm a PA in a legal firm specialising in civil, criminal and family law. We have an unwritten dress code of dark suit and blouse, which is fine by me. It takes the decision of what to wear every day pretty much out of my hands. I lay my outfit out before I go to bed each night in an effort to shave a few minutes off my routine and give me more pillow time. On autopilot, I pull on my clothes, brush my hair into some sort of top knot – the success of which varies daily – and I'm ready to rock. I never wear make-up. That would involve too much complication at this time of day and I'd probably go out looking like a pantomime dame. I try to convince myself that natural is best and that in years to come I'll be reaping the benefits for not having put all that stuff on my face. That's my theory, anyway.

On my way downstairs, I pass Finn's bedroom and poke my head inside. In the gloom, all I can see is a heap in the middle of the bed. My darling boy has never been a tidy sleeper. He's fifteen now, but I still think of him as my baby. You always do, don't you?

Braving the ripe fug of a teenage boy's bedroom, I tiptoe in, crossing the minefield of discarded clothes, trainers and PlayStation games. Despite my best efforts Finn's bedroom has remained steadfastly untidy since he was about seven. In all other ways, he's been a model child, so I cut him some slack and only insist on a quarterly fumigation. I go to sit beside him on the bed. His mop of dark hair is just visible above the duvet. I plant a kiss on it.

'Muuuuum,' he complains sleepily.

'I'm just leaving, sweetheart. I'll see you tonight.'

'OK.'

'Don't be late for school.'

'I've had a headache all night,' he says, still drowsy. 'Can I stay off today?'

'Come on,' I urge. 'You've had so much time off, Finn. I had a letter from the headmaster about it last week. You need to get yourself up and out. You'll feel better after a shower and I'll leave a couple of paracetamol on the table for you. Pops will come round at eight to do your breakfast.'

'He doesn't need to.'

'I know. But he likes it. And it makes me feel better too. Deal?'

Finn nods and snuggles down again. I stroke his hair. Sometimes I worry about him. He's not a robust child. He's not one of these hulking great teenagers with shoulders like prop forwards that you see at the school gates towering over the teachers. Finn is small, slender and never has much appetite. He seems to be plagued by a constant stream of minor infections and headaches. If he catches a cold, he never seems to shrug it off and it can last up to a month. He seems to live on antibiotics and, surely, that can't be right. Recently, he's had so many days off that the school are getting quite grumpy about it. I've asked him if he's being bullied or if there's another reason why he doesn't want to go in, but he says not.

'I've got to go.'

'Have a good day,' he murmurs.

'You too. You've done all your homework?'

'Sort of.'

'Oh, Finn. I'm hoping you're going to become a brain surgeon or something and keep your old mum in the style she'd like to become accustomed to.'

'I'm not sure some half-completed course work on the Rise of the Roman Empire is going to make any difference to me getting me there.' He looks up at me from beneath the covers and grins.

My heart melts. It's been just me and Finn for a long time now and we're a tight little unit of two. I probably should be more strict as a parent but he knows and I know that I'm a complete pushover when it comes to him.

'Besides, we're just going over old stuff now for the exams. We're not learning anything new.'

'At least try. Don't ever regret not doing your best.'

'OK.'

'I'll feed the fiends before I go. Don't let them do the starving animal routine on you and get two breakfasts.'

'I'll do it. You'll miss your coach.'

I glance at my watch. He's right.

'Thanks, love. You're a star. Be ready for when Pops comes.' And, with a final kiss, I head out to face another day.

Chapter Two

The coach stops at the corner of my road and, as I get there, I see it trundling towards me. It's big, shiny, blue and very comfortable, but I loathe the sight of it nevertheless. My fellow commuters are waiting here too, huddled on the pavement, and I nod hello to them. Despite some of us having commuted together for several years, we don't generally speak to each other. Well, only in times of crisis. If the bus is late or the weather is particularly bad, we all have a good moan then.

At ten to six there aren't many other people about and the usually busy street has a pleasant stillness about it. As it's the tail end of March, it's also about half an hour before sunrise but it's heartening to know that the dark days of winter are behind us and the mornings are getting a little bit lighter with every passing day. Soon I won't be leaving in the dark and coming home in it too.

This is not the best area, but it's not the worst either. I live in a nice Victorian terraced house. Not one of the ones with original sash windows and a slate roof – no one thought to make this a conservation area – but rather one which has been modernised with UPVC windows from Zenith or someone and has had all the fireplaces taken out. It's not one with huge rooms and high ceilings either, but is a small, modest abode. However, the kitchen is big enough to fit a table in, which is its saving grace and a boon for an addictive crafter like me, as the dining room table is usually swamped with paper, glitter and stuff. At least we have somewhere else to eat our meals rather than on our knees with trays in front of the telly – though I do favour a bit of that sometimes.

The bus pulls up and we all file on. Despite not having allocated seats, we all sit in the same place every day and God help anyone who goes off piste and decides to try another seat. The looks! They say that they can't kill, but I think they can come pretty close. My personal Seat of Choice is left-hand side at the back just in front of the gap for the rear emergency door. That way nobody is sitting directly behind me. No knees in the back. No snoring if someone nods off. There's only one stop before mine, so it's more often than not free but, if someone else tries to make a bid for it and is already sitting there, I am totally screwed for the entire day. Nothing else goes right.

'Morning, Christie,' Toni says as I take my seat. She's been the morning assistant on this coach for nearly as long as I've been travelling. 'Usual for you?'

She hardly needs to ask. I prefer an extra five minutes in bed to breakfast at home, so I always have two strong cups of coffee on my journey to kick-start my engine. As soon as we set off, she bustles about serving us all our warm drinks with a cheery smile.

'No Susan?' she adds as she pours.

'No.' My new morning run coach companion hasn't turned up today and there's an empty seat beside me. 'She said she had a sore throat yesterday. Maybe she's come down with a cold.'

'Seems like a nice lady.' She hands me my coffee and I tip up my two quid. But that does include a free refill.

'Yes.' Susan has already demonstrated admirably that she

understands commuting etiquette and keeps chat to a minimum, respecting the need for peace and quiet. The only time that a buzz of whispers goes round the bus is when Toni checks the tickets and someone is caught on the fiddle. Thankfully, she has the sense to give us all coffee before she checks the tickets. The good ladies and gentlemen of the commuter coach couldn't cope with a scandal with low caffeine levels.

'Ted in the office told me that she's just bought an annual season ticket, so it looks as if we'll be seeing more of her,' Toni confides.

'That's good.'

Toni nods at my cup. 'Give me a shout when you're ready for your top-up.' Then she moves onto the next seat.

The coach is always cosy and warm and sometimes, if I'm lucky or particularly knackered, I manage to catch up on another hour or so of sleep before we hit London. I nurse my cup with its cardboard jacket and pop in my earphones. I'm listening to an audio book. Chick lit. It's the closest I ever get to romance these days.

We swing onto the A5 and head towards Hockliffe, our next passenger pick-up point. I settle down and close my eyes and let the words of the narrator wash over me.

My ex-husband Liam Chapman and I divorced five years ago now. It sounds strange to say this, but there was nothing really wrong with our relationship. Our only crime was to marry too young. There was no big drama, no other person on the side-lines, it was just that I don't believe we'd ever really been in love. Not properly. We liked each other well enough and we'd been together since we were fifteen, so we didn't really know any different. We were so comfortable together that we just assumed that the next step was to get married and so we did. Yet, even on my wedding day, I didn't feel any great rush of love and that's not right, is it?

Liam worked in the hospitality industry – managing a chain hotel in Milton Keynes – and, eventually, was offered a job overseas. A new hotel complex in Dubai needed a general manager. It was at that point we both stopped to question where we were going. He was desperate to take it. The job was a big promotion and came with a nice, fat salary – tax-free – paid-for accommodation and a dozen other perks that I can't even remember now. The very thought made my blood run cold. I was as reluctant as Liam was keen. It just seemed like too much upheaval. Finn would have been starting secondary school within the year. It would have taken me away from my parents who are, and have always been, my lifeline. Liam would have been working long hours and it wasn't guaranteed that I'd get a work permit, so I could have been stuck at home all day. Liam wanted to get out of Wolverton and see more of the world. I liked the fact that I knew everyone in the local shops – still do – and a week in Cornwall every year is enough of the world for me. The more he pleaded, the more I could see it wouldn't work. When it came down to it I realised that, although I really liked him a lot, I didn't love him enough to turn my world upside down for him. I didn't want to go to Dubai. And, more importantly, I didn't really want to go to Dubai with Liam.

We both cried a lot when we reached our final decision. I would stay here and Liam would go. There were lots of promises about him coming home regularly and talk that Finn wouldn't miss out as he'd Skype him every day and we could both fly out to the hotel for regular holidays. And I'm sure we both meant it.

I went to my parents' house and drank tea and talked about the weather while my husband packed up and left our lives. Within a month of him going, he'd met someone else who adored him. Of course he did. Essentially, he's a nice man. We divorced without fuss and Liam remarried. He has a lovely wife called

Jodie and, now, five years or so later, they have two small children of their own. He sends us money regularly. Not that much, if I'm honest, but it all helps. I can't fault him for that. However, though they do keep in touch, the daily Skype sessions with Finn never quite materialised and, to date, he's never been there on holiday. Liam has made a few flying visits home, but it's not really enough. He never forgets Finn's birthday or Christmas, so that's some small comfort. It doesn't seem to bother my son – my dear old dad has seamlessly stepped into the parenting role for him – but I do wonder if it plays on his mind.

The coach draws into the coach stop at Hockliffe, just before we turn towards Toddington to hit the motorway and join the endless stream of traffic heading south into the city. I clear a patch in the condensation on the window and scan the people who are waiting without really seeing them. In this day and age, you do think that it would be possible for more people to work from home than join this tedious daily exodus to the big smoke. What's the point of all these advances in technology if it can't even achieve that? Toni comes and lifts her coffee pot and an enquiring eyebrow. I take the lid off my cup and hold it out for a refill.

When she moves off to the next passenger, a man flops down into the seat next me. He throws his bag on the floor. Clearly he doesn't realise that this is now Susan's seat. Although, admittedly, she still has quite a slim claim on it. I haven't seen his face before and I have to admit that it's quite a nice face. Even at this hour in the morning, I register that.

'Phew,' he says. 'That was a bit of a rush. I cut it too fine today. I can see that I'm going to have to get up earlier in the morning. Snatching that last five minutes was a mistake.'

'A man after my own heart,' I quip.

The doors close and we set off again towards the M1.

'I'm Henry,' he says holding out a hand. 'Henry Jackson.'

'Pleased to meet you. Christie Chapman.'

'First day at a new job,' he tells me. 'Bit nervous. First-time commuter too. Is it hideous?'

'Yes.'

He laughs at that, as if I'm joking. People are looking round to see who, other than Toni, has the temerity to be quite so chirpy at this hour.

As I noted, Henry Jackson is not a bad-looking bloke. Not that I'm any kind of judge of these things. He's a bit dishevelled, but then he did say that he got ready in a rush. One side of his shirt collar is turned up and his tie's not quite straight. His hair is dark and wavy and looks as if he hasn't got round to combing it yet. And it needs a cut. But when he turns to smile at me again, I see that he's got nice teeth and rather kind grey eyes. Hmm. It's a long time since I've noticed the colour of anyone's eyes.

'Tea or coffee, love?' Toni asks.

'Tea, please.' His accent is northern. Manchester or somewhere. Flat vowels. 'This is very civilised.'

She pours him a cup and moves on to bring joy in the way of beverages to the new arrivals.

'Have you been doing this for years?' he asks.

It doesn't seem the right time to tell him that the first rule of commuting is minimal conversation.

'It's quite exciting,' he adds without waiting for my reply. He takes in his surroundings. 'Where did you get on?'

Giving up with my audio book, I pull out my earphones and say, 'Wolverton.'

'I'm new to the area,' Henry Jackson tells me. 'Where's that?'

This one's obviously going to be a talker. I hope we're not on the same coach home otherwise I'll never find out if the dappy heroine falls into bed with a man who is quite clearly unsuitable.

Chapter Three

My office is on the Embankment and the firm I work for is ancient – started in the year dot or something. On the other hand, our offices are bright and contemporary and are full of fancy artworks. The old guard has pretty much been pensioned off and are probably now spending their cossetted retirement at the second homes in Spain, so all the partners in the firm are currently younger than me. Such is the way of the world. The new bunch are all kindness itself though. Maybe because they are hotshot lawyers and realise they could get their arses sued off if they were mean to their employees.

I work for five lawyers, all men except for Robyn Reynolds who has been at the firm almost as long as I have. Robyn joined straight from university as an intern, then did her training here and has, over the course of the last eighteen years or so, worked her way up to being a senior partner. Whereas, in the same space of time, I have worked my way up from being a secretary to a PA. Hmm.

For my sins, I organise their travel, conferences and meetings, talk to counsels' clerks, sort out billing and put together trial bundles for hearings. I also have the world's most complex telephone with so many buttons that I still haven't managed to work out what they all do. We have a big television screen in the office too that's always, quite depressingly, set to Sky news.

'Morning, Christie.' Robyn is already lurking by my work-station. 'You're looking frazzled. Traffic bad?'

'No.' I strip off my coat. 'I had a talker on the coach. Missed two hours of beauty sleep.'

'A talker. How rude.'

'He's northern. Doesn't understand that people in the south don't speak to each other on public transport.'

'He'll learn.'

'It felt mean to tell him to shut up. So I now know that he's divorced. Recently. Moved down here from Manchester for a new start.' Go me on spotting the accent. 'He's starting a new job today in publishing.'

'Hot?'

I shrug.

'That's not an absolute no.'

'Quite handsome, I'd say. But I didn't really look that much. I just wanted him to shut up so I could go back to my book.'

'Wild night on the tiles?'

'Yes. Went to a rave, popped a load of e's and got shit-faced. Didn't bother going to bed, just came straight here.'

We both roll our eyes at the ludicrous nature of my answer. I don't even know if those are the right terms these days.

'I was up late, making a nice birthday card for my friend.'

'Ah. Crazy fool.' Robyn is well aware that my life is one long trip to the fun palace. 'Sit. I'll get you a coffee.' She heads off to the machine.

This is no time to remind her that, generally, the PA gets the coffee for the boss. But this is why I love Robyn so much. She's not afraid to get her hands dirty in the coffee department. She's also smart, savvy and is a player. Whereas I am not. I don't have a law degree either, but that's by the by. Some days, I feel as if I do.

Although we're pretty much the same age, we couldn't be more different. She is tall, athletic, blonde. I am not. She has one of those sharp, chippy haircuts that I so desire. Robyn spends hours in the gym working out. I do not. At lunchtime she eats alfalfa sprouts or some such from our posh restaurant on the thirteenth floor. I nip to Tesco and get their three quid meal deal. I have a cheese sandwich, a bag of crisps and a diet Pepsi. She drinks Phresh Greens to keep the pH of her body in balance or some swamp-coloured smoothie she makes herself which she calls Warrior Juice, which – quite frankly – just sounds pervy. I prefer to go down the vodka and Red Bull route. Robyn also has a lesbian lover and I definitely do not. Though she often tries to persuade me that going over to the pink side was the best thing she ever did.

The Robster puts my coffee down and perches on the corner of my desk. I move papers about and try to remember what I was doing yesterday. 'Have you ever considered green tea?'

'No.'

'I worry about your caffeine intake.'

'So do I,' I say. 'I don't get nearly enough to keep me focused.'

She rolls her eyes. 'Imogen said thank you for the anniversary card, by the way.'

'I can't believe it's a year.'

'Me neither.'

Robyn married her partner, Imogen, in a lovely ceremony in the Westminster register office and then had a reception on a boat on the Thames. I organised most of it for her. When I say organised it, that might be bigging up my part. I was the go-between with her uber efficient and slightly scary wedding planner, Cressida – who we all nicknamed Cruella. When she barked orders, I did her bidding. At Robyn and Imogen's request,

I did make the invitations, place cards and more than my fair share of decorations – miles of personalised bunting and the like. I was so pleased – and relieved – how well they came out.

It was a glorious day. No expense spared. Imogen – now Mrs Reynolds – is also tall and blonde. She's a fêted interior designer and is as rich as Croesus. They live together in the swankiest house I've ever seen in Hampstead and throw an annual star-studded garden party for Imo's clients who are mainly people from the reality soaps and footballers' wives who I never recognise.

I might be small, on the curvy side due to never letting an alfalfa sprout pass my lips, and be somewhat challenged in the climbing the career ladder area, but I do have a fantastic son, a tiny house that would benefit from Imogen's attentions, and a great family. Robyn does not. She's desperate for kids, but it's just not happening for them despite half a dozen different attempts at IVF. One has no eggs left at all, the other is starting an early menopause – which just seems like too much bad luck. I keep trying to get them to consider pets, but they find the thought of pet hair in their minimalist home abhorrent. Quite how they'd cope with kids running around is another matter.

'Imo says that you're wasted here,' Robyn says as she sips her brew. 'You should be doing something artistic.'

'I take that as a compliment.'

'Imogen is A Woman Who Knows.'

She is. There's a long list of eminent and upcoming artists who are among their friends. Even after the success of their wedding decorations, I was slightly terrified when Robyn asked me to make her an anniversary card. It's never just a card for either of them. It took me three nights to get it right. Robyn even took a snip of each of their Alice Temperley wedding dresses – inside the hem – so that I could use it in the design. Despite the angst, I have to say that I was rather pleased with the result.

'She says that you don't charge enough.'

To be honest, if I had to charge by the hour it would be the most expensive anniversary card on the planet. 'It's not about the money,' I say. 'I didn't want to charge you anything at all. You know that.'

'Nonsense,' Robyn says. 'Don't underestimate your talent.'

'It's just hard to make any serious dosh from arts and crafts. Not unless you're Kirsty Allsopp and are all over the telly.'

I spend my entire lunchtime at work online looking at craft bits and bobs – while eating my unhealthy cheese sandwich and bag of crisps and avoiding Robyn's sideways glances. Sometimes she mouths 'NutriBullet' at me and I mouth back 'Sod off.'

Mostly, I make cards for friends and colleagues. It's hardly going to buy me a Learjet or a top-of-the-range Merc, but it brings in a bit of pin money and covers – mostly – the cost of my crafting addiction. Unless I have a particularly mad splurge on eBay, of course. Frankly, you can never have too many crystals or decorative mini-clothes pegs.

I'd always dabbled with crafts, but I guess I started doing it in earnest when Liam first left. What can you do at night on your own when you've got a child upstairs in bed? You can't go out gallivanting. You can't crank the music up. I could only prevail on my dear parents to babysit for Finn every so often while I had a wild night on two glasses of wine at the local pub with my girlfriends. Finn never much cared for me leaving him. My son liked it best when we were snuggled up on the sofa together with the fur babies, even when he hit his teens, and, frankly, I did nothing to discourage it. There was never really the spare money either. We're not exactly on the breadline, but by the time I've paid for all the household bills, Finn's school stuff, my crafting addiction and food for several more animals than is strictly necessary, there's not much left to splash around.

Plus – dare I say it – I quite like being at home on my own sofa. I'm not a natural goer-outer. However, I'm not the sort of person who can sit still just watching soaps. I like to be doing something with my hands. Over the years, I've knitted, crocheted, embroidered and cross-stitched. I get it all from my mum. She's always been keen on home-made crafts. I don't think I had one school uniform which Mum hadn't run up on her Singer sewing machine. She had a few little craft businesses herself over the years too. When Care Bears were all the rage, our dining room was wall-to-wall fur fabric as Mum fashioned Birthday Bear, Bedtime Bear, Funshine Bear *et al*. When I got home from school, I was paid a very poor piece-work rate to stuff them with kapok filling and put their eyes in. If you wanted pocket money in our house, you had to earn it.

I do a bit of a craft blog too. Nothing much. I put up my projects and a bit of blah-blah. I don't do it every day either – just as and when I can. I'm amazed that anyone follows me, but they do. I keep thinking that I could do some videos and maybe become an internet sensation like PewDiePie or Zoella or Pointless Alfie. Maybe not. For a start, I'm sort of twenty years too old. I don't think there are that many middle-aged internet sensations. Certainly not in the craft world.

While I'm thinking about all this, Robyn drains her cup. 'Well, we've got work to do, Christie. What shall we start on first? Do you fancy typing up some affidavits or tackling the month end billing?'

'Your call. You're the boss.'

'Oh, yeah,' she says. 'You can do the next coffee run.'

'Now?'

'Why not?' she agrees. 'Let's not be too hasty about these things. We should *ease* ourselves into the day.'

I'm seeing nothing to argue with here.

Keep an eye out for Carole Matthews'
new festive and romantic novel,

Christmas Cakes and Mistletoe Nights

You won't want to miss it – out October 2017!

**Join Fay and her friends this Christmas and indulge in this
wonderful, cake-filled novel of romance and friendship.**

Fay and Danny are madly in love and it's all Fay's ever dreamed
of. But she left everything – including the delightful cake shop
she used to run – to be with Danny on his cosy canal boat *The
Dreamcatcher*. And as she soon finds out, making delicious
cakes on the water isn't always smooth sailing!

Then Fay gets a call from her friends, a call that sends her
back to where it all began, back to where she first met
Danny, back to her friends and the Cake Shop in the Garden.
It will be hard being away from Danny but their relationship
is strong enough to survive . . . isn't it?

Fay soon falls happily back in love with her passion for
baking – especially now she's on dry land again! – and starts
to wonder if she ever should have left. With Christmas
around the corner, Fay is determined that her friends will
have a very merry time, but does that mean even more time
away from Danny? Can Fay really get everything she ever
wanted in *Christmas Cakes and Mistletoe Nights*?